DINOSAUR

S T A K E O U T

DINOSAUR

S T A K E O U T

JUDITH SILVERTHORNE

Edited by Barbara Sapergia.
Cover illustrations by Aries Cheung.
Cover and book design by Duncan Campbell.
Printed and bound in Canada at Gauvin Press.

National Library of Canada Cataloguing in Publication Data

Silverthorne, Judith, date-
Dinosaur stakeout / Judith Silverthorne.

(Dinosaur adventure series ; 3)
Includes bibliographical references.
ISBN 1-55050-344-8

I. Dinosaurs—Juvenile fiction. I. Title. II. Series:
Silverthorne, Judith, date— Dinosaur adventure series ; 3.

PS8587.I2763D57 2006   jC813'.54   C2006-901289-X

10 9 8 7 6 5 4 3 2 1

2517 Victoria Ave
Regina, Saskatchewan
Canada   S4P OT2

available in Canada and the US from:
Fitzhenry & Whiteside
195 Allstate Parkway
Markham, Ontario
Canada   L3R 4T8

The publisher gratefully acknowledges the financial assistance of the Saskatchewan Arts Board, the Canada Council for the Arts, including the Millennium Arts Fund, the Government of Canada through the Book Publishing Industry Development Program (BPIDP), Association for the Export of Canadian Books, and the City of Regina Arts Commission, for its publishing program.

As always to my son, Aaron,
who inspired me with this series
from the beginning.

To Danion and Modeste
for their enthusiasm and support

In memory of Blackie and Wild Bill.

CHAPTER ONE

Daniel bolted upright before the six a.m. alarm rang. Daylight streamed across his bed through the slits in the blinds. Without hesitation, he threw the covers off and limped into the bathroom as fast as he could to beat the rest of his family. Today, the first of the tourists would be arriving at their dinosaur dig operation, and he didn't want to miss a thing!

The idea for a tourist business had begun a year and a half earlier when the Bringhams' reclusive neighbour, Ole Pederson, had located an almost complete *Edmontosaurus* skeleton right on the border of their adjoining property. Daniel had helped with this important find and other fossils they'd unearthed too. Their discoveries had been housed in the Climax museum soon afterwards so the public could view them.

A short time later, he and Mr. Pederson had campaigned for a paleontology tourist operation with Daniel's parents. They agreed the plan would be a great way to bring much-needed income to help them keep their farm. Then the Lindstroms, his best friend Jed's family, had become partners in it too. Tourists could visit a real dig, stay for lunch, or even camp overnight in the new campground the two families had built.

Stepping into the shower stall, Daniel groaned. He clung to the towel rod as the water cascaded over him, trying to avoid getting the scrapes on his head wet. He examined the abrasions on his arms and legs and the long scratch across his chest. He thought again of the past few days and how the bullying Nelwin brothers – Craig and Todd – had caused many of his injuries. Of course, tussling with dinosaurs hadn't helped any, but he hadn't told his parents that part of the story. Who would believe that he'd been flung into prehistoric time?

It was bad enough that the Nelwins had attacked him and tried to destroy his secret hideout. Their jealousy over his and Ole Pederson's previous paleontology finds – and the special recognition that resulted – had boiled over the day before. They'd caused some serious damage to his hideout and to his parents' property too. The worst thing was that they'd been hurled into the time of the dinosaurs with him, and now they were in on his secret.

Daniel had acquired a piece of redwood bark a few days earlier when he'd been unexpectedly transported back in time to the Cretaceous Period, and he'd learned that even a small object from that time had the power to send him back to the era of the dinosaurs. He'd hidden the bark in his hideout, but the Nelwins had uncovered it as they tried to wreck Daniel's belongings. When Daniel had grabbed Craig to keep him from touching it, Todd had seized his arm. They'd all connected when Craig touched the bark, and found themselves instantly thrown back to a dangerous prehistoric world.

The Nelwins couldn't believe it. They'd thought Daniel had tricked them somehow, and Craig wouldn't give him the piece of bark – their only way to get back to their own time. Only after a *Troodon* ripped a chunk out of Daniel's pant leg and a *Tyrannosaurus rex* tried to eat them for dinner had Daniel been able to convince Craig to give up the piece of bark. Even so, at the last moment a *Dromaeosaurus* narrowly missed slashing Daniel's chest open. So much for his trying to save the Nelwins! He shuddered again as he remembered the harrowing experience.

Once they'd returned safely, Daniel demanded that the Nelwins restore his hideout and swore them to secrecy about its location. He also secured Pederson and Jed's silence about their time travel adventures.

Back at home, Daniel's family decided to drop the charges of vandalism against the Nelwin brothers in exchange for restitution. This meant they would have to work off the damage they'd done around the farm and at the campground after they'd cleaned up Daniel's hideout. They also had to help Daniel with his barn chores, because he'd been hurt when they pushed him down a hillside in a barrel during their rampage.

They had seemed contrite enough the evening before, but would Craig and Todd keep up their end of the bargain and show up for work today?

By the time Daniel dressed, he could hear his mom rattling breakfast dishes in the kitchen. She had worked some of her nursing wonders on him the night before, and his scrapes and cuts were already beginning to heal over. Even his leg seemed to have limbered with the hot water from the shower and his moving about. As he stepped into the hallway, he met his dad with a fresh towel slung over his shoulder, heading for the bathroom.

"I can see you don't need any prodding to do your chores this morning, son!" Dad's dark eyes rested on him with affection. He tousled Daniel's hair, avoiding the painful areas on his head.

Daniel grinned and headed towards the stairs. When Dad had safely closed the bathroom door, Daniel slid down the banister, and with a *thunk* landed on the floor at the bottom.

"Daniel!" Mom said, with a warning raise of her eyebrows.

"It's easier, Mom!" He pointed to his sore leg.

She shook her head and popped the batter-filled muffin pans into the oven. "We don't need you falling on your noggin too!"

Daniel headed out the door to do his barn chores. As he made his way across the yard, the twittering of the sparrows in the caragana hedge signalled a perfect July day. A gentle breeze ruffled his still damp dark hair and there wasn't a cloud in the bright blue morning sky. Dactyl, his golden retriever named after the prehistoric pterodactyl, dashed across the yard towards him. Daniel sank slowly down on one knee to pet him, then continued on his way.

With each step, he studied the ground and thought of the many layers of rock underneath him, which designated the various geological ages of the earth towards its molten centre. The one he was most keenly interested in – the Cretaceous Period – lay only a few metres below his feet. A flush of excitement coursed through him as he recalled the fantastic things he'd discovered in that prehistoric world. He got goosebumps just thinking of what fossils might lie beneath where he walked. If only he could explore more of it.

Once at the barnyard, he herded the two milk cows into the barn, luring them with a ready pail of chop – today, just crushed oats – from the feed room right inside the barn. He fed and watered the two animals, then eased himself carefully onto the milking stool by their prize Holstein, Lily. As he leaned his head against her soft belly and began milking her, the Nelwin brothers entered the barn. They already knew what they were supposed to do. Daniel watched to see how they'd do it.

Todd, a strapping sixteen-year-old with dark, bristly hair, grunted hello to Daniel. Snatching up a pitchfork, he moved into a newly vacated stall where he hoisted manure onto the stoneboat parked in the middle of the barn. He attacked the muck in short rapid movements as if he was afraid of being reprimanded for not doing the work fast enough.

Craig shuffled behind his brother, sullenly letting his shoulder-length brown hair fall over his eyes. The stocky fifteen-year-old nodded at Daniel as he picked up a second fork and began cleaning out a stall.

They all worked quietly for a few minutes. The only sounds came from the scraping of pitchforks on the wooden floor, the *squirt, squirt* of milk hitting the metal pail, and the soft mews of the kittens as they chased one another through the loose straw. Dust motes floated in the air, caught on the sunbeams flowing from a high, small window. Daniel glanced over at the brothers across the barn in the subdued light of the interior. He could see they'd rolled up their sleeves and were working industriously.

When he was done milking Lily, Daniel gave her a pat on the rump and moved over to Daisy. Robotically, he milked the second cow while she stood placidly chewing her cud. A few moments later, Dactyl came through the open sliding door to investigate. He sniffed Todd and Craig all over as they petted him eagerly, then he wandered about the barn examining the stalls.

"Dactyl!" Daniel called softly.

Wagging his tail happily, Dactyl came over and licked Daniel's face. Daniel gave Dactyl a nudge with his shoulder and continued milking Daisy. His pet wandered back outside, and gave chase to some crows that had landed on a nearby fencepost. From the pasture just beyond the barn, Gypsy, his grey pinto mare, whinnied anxiously for her breakfast.

Daniel's stomach rumbled too and he quickly finished milking. Releasing Lily and Daisy to wander back into the fenced part of the farmyard, he stepped outside to pour some milk into an old tin saucer for the kittens and Marble, the mother cat. Then he dropped the pails of milk inside the separating room. With a quick backward glance at the Nelwins, he walked outside to feed Gypsy and the older horse, Pepper.

When Daniel headed back to the separating room, a shaft of daylight shone across Todd and Craig. Daniel looked more closely at the pair and noticed there were bruises on Craig's arms. He approached the brothers, who were talking together, but as he drew closer, they went silent again. At least they were keeping up their end of the work bargain so far. What was going on with them wasn't any of his business.

Some minutes later, Daniel finished separating the milk. Dismantling the machine, he left the components to soak in the hot water provided by Dad earlier. Mom would finish washing them later when she fed the chickens and gathered eggs. When she had to be at work at the hospital early, these tasks became Daniel's, and he was relieved that he didn't have to do them today. Many families in the community just bought milk products and eggs at the store, but the Bringhams preferred fresh, home-produced foods wherever possible.

"I'm going in for breakfast now," Daniel said, carrying the pails of milk and cream to the door. The boys continued to work, barely acknowledging him.

Suddenly, a thought struck him. He turned back to the brothers. "Have you eaten?"

More mumbles came from the brothers with a general nod of their heads that Daniel could only take to mean they had. Thoughtfully, Daniel limped across the yard towards the house. How had Craig got the bruises?

In the kitchen, he sat down beside Cheryl in her high chair and helped himself to muffins and chunks of juicy cantaloupe. Shortly afterwards, Dad came in and joined them at the table. Cheryl poked at the muffin, broke a piece off and popped it into her mouth, then offered a chunk to Daniel, her blue eyes sparkling with mischief. She laughed as he took a big bite and chomped it down.

There was a knock on the door and Ole Pederson appeared. He was clean-shaven and his white wisps of hair were patted down. His grey eyes twinkled with anticipation.

"Anything for you, Ole?" Mom asked.

"Just coffee," he answered, sitting next to Daniel. "Had breakfast some time ago."

As Mom poured the steaming brown liquid, she glanced out the window at the sound of a tractor starting up.

"That'll be the Nelwins hauling the stoneboat to the manure pile," Dad said, without getting up to look. "They're done in good time."

"Guess it makes a difference with three of you doing the work." Mom smiled at Daniel.

He nodded with a wry look on his face. "Sure is a hard way to get some help!" Daniel declared, pointing to his bruises, as they all laughed.

"Do you know if they've had breakfast?" Mom asked Daniel.

"I think so," he answered, passing the plate of fruit to Mr. Pederson. "At least, that's what they said."

Without a word, Mom poured juice into two disposable glasses, grabbed a couple of serviettes, and a paper plate, placed four muffins and a stack of fruit on it, and headed out the door. Dad and Ole Pederson didn't seem to notice. Daniel stared after her with curiosity.

A few minutes later, he peeked out the window and saw Mom heading back to the house empty-handed. So the Nelwins hadn't eaten breakfast after all.

When Daniel's mom reappeared in the kitchen, he thought she looked upset.

"Something wrong, Libby?" Daniel's dad asked.

"It's the Nelwins. I don't think they had any breakfast before they left."

"That's not good. We'll have to feed them well when they're working here."

"Yes," she said, "we can certainly do that."

Pederson addressed Daniel. "So, you all set to go?"

"You bet!"

Dad consulted a sheet of paper at his elbow. "The first guests will be here in an hour or so. They're doing the quarry tour, and some hikes, and are camping here tonight."

"How many are there?" asked Daniel.

"Looks like two adults and their two young children."

"Piece of cake!" said Daniel. He thought about his best friend Jed and his sister Lucy, coming to help as guides.

"Yes, but there are twenty other groups coming throughout the day!"

"Whoa!" Daniel took the last bite of his muffin. All three of them would be busy keeping track of the visitors, while the adults did their respective jobs.

Dad continued reading down the list as they finished their breakfast.

"Most are staying over," he said. "Then there are the ones that may just drop in."

"We have our work cut out for us today!" Ole Pederson said. "So let's get to it!" He downed the last of his coffee and shuffled to his feet.

Daniel felt the excitement ripple through his body.

Sharing their paleontological finds with others was a thrill, although maybe not as exhilarating as seeing the creatures in the flesh. He had learned a great deal about dinosaurs by flipping into prehistoric time and would love to know more, but he could do without the danger. Going to the ancient past again was out of the question anyway – since he'd tossed away the scrap of redwood bark on his last trip. He had no way to get back, and no way to return. Still, a little part of his adventurous spirit wished he could find a way to go back one more time. The rest of him was relieved it could never happen again.

CHAPTER TWO

"**A** penny for your thoughts," said Ole Pederson when they stepped into the bright sunshine of the farmyard. Dad had stayed behind to have a last minute conversation with Mom, so they were alone.

"Just thinking about seeing live dinosaurs," Daniel said quietly.

Pederson cocked his head and waited for Daniel to continue.

"Mr. Pederson, do you believe I've been going back to prehistoric time?" Daniel asked tentatively.

The old man took his time responding, as they sauntered over to his old Studebaker truck.

"I don't know what to think, Daniel. I can't imagine how you could have. Yet you certainly experienced something. Do *you* think it was real?"

"Sure felt like it," answered Daniel. "It was just like you and I standing here now. I've had dreams, but they weren't that vivid." He eyed Mr. Pederson, waiting for his reaction.

"I've never experienced anything like it, but this old world is a strange place and I've always tried to keep an open mind. So I suppose, why not this?" said Pederson, unloading the equipment he'd take with him for the day.

"I can't think of any other likely explanation," said Daniel, watching the old man. He was pretty sure Pederson believed him.

Pederson raised his eyebrows. "Indeed, how would you have acquired some of those cuts and bruises during your episode otherwise? The Nelwins sure aren't responsible for all of them. I know it's not your imagination and you surely couldn't do that to yourself."

He patted Daniel on the shoulder. "I never would have thought it possible. But I'm glad that's behind us and it won't happen again."

"Me too," replied Daniel, feeling happy and relieved now that his friend and mentor accepted the truth about his travels. Then he looked at Mr. Pederson and asked, "Would you have liked to go, if you'd had the chance?"

"Who wouldn't want to explore knowledge like that first-hand?" Mr. Pederson hoisted his pack onto his back. "But this is a great time to experience too, lad."

Then, drawing his arm across the skyline encompassing the farmyard, the campsite, and the direction of the quarry, he said, "This quarry operation is enough of an accomplishment for me."

Pederson adjusted his backpack and they stood in companionable silence, each lost in his own thoughts.

Moments later, the Lindstrom family pulled into the driveway. They parked their bright red Chevrolet Silverado crew-cab truck in the shade behind the combination outdoor kitchen and snack bar. Jed's family poured out of the truck, all chattering at once. Dactyl barked excitedly, running from one to another, wagging his tail.

Mom came from the house with a huge coffee urn, headed for the outdoor kitchen. Greta Lindstrom, Jed's mom, followed from the truck with large plastic containers of baking. The two youngest daughters, Leanne and Lindsay, came behind with bags of groceries containing fresh fruit, vegetables, homemade bread, and assorted condiments. Lucy carried a portfolio under her arm, and she and Jed joined Daniel and Mr. Pederson.

They could see Jed's dad, Doug Lindstrom, coming slowly down the road in a beat-up old jeep with a string of trotting quarter horses tied behind. These gentle animals would be used for the tourists, while the guides rode Gypsy or Pepper. When Doug Lindstrom arrived in the yard, Dad jumped into the jeep with him and they drove at a snail's pace down the winding trail towards the campsite halfway down the valley. Meanwhile, Ole Pederson gathered Daniel, Jed, and Lucy around him.

"All right, team, are you ready to go?" Ole Pederson asked, eyeing each of them. "Lucy, tourist maps and info sheets?"

Lucy opened up the satchel and held up a sheaf of papers. "Ready!"

"Check!" said Pederson. "Jed?"

"Ready to go, sir!" He dug a piece of paper out of his pocket and unfolded it to reveal a map with special markings on it. The plan was to give their guests the best view and include botanical sights along the way, while at the same time preserving the natural habitat.

Pederson nodded at Jed. "Good!"

Then he turned to Daniel with a twinkle in his eyes. "I already know you're revved up!"

"Who's taking the first group?" Lucy asked, turning businesslike.

"That will depend on what the guests want – if they're hiking on foot, or want the horseback trail – and what all of you decide." Pederson replied. He obviously didn't want to choose between them.

"I'll go over the information and rules with them," Lucy volunteered. "Then if either Jed or Daniel wants to take them, that's okay with me."

"Why don't you take them, Jed?" Daniel offered. "I have to get the Nelwins started at cleaning my hideout."

"You're sure?" Jed said eagerly, tucking in his shirt and patting down his fair curly hair.

Daniel nodded. He could see the Nelwins out of the corner of his eye. Todd jumped off the parked tractor as he approached, and Craig closed the barn door firmly. "You'll do fine! I'll be just a whistle away."

The three guides had devised a sequence of whistling with their fingers to alert each other when they needed help. Pederson also had a code, if he needed them.

"All right, I'm heading off to the dig," Pederson said. "I'll see you there soon, Jed. And the rest of you later."

Pederson strode off to his truck to pick up the remainder of his gear. Jed and Lucy headed for the outdoor kitchen to help where they could. Mom crossed the yard to the henhouse, egg basket in hand. Daniel headed towards the Nelwins.

"All done the barn chores?" Daniel inquired pleasantly when he joined them.

"Yeah," Todd said. His stance suggested he had better things to do, but would tolerate Daniel.

Craig joined them, his head hung low. He wouldn't look Daniel in the eyes.

"What do you have planned for us next?" Todd asked somewhat sourly.

"Hey, I didn't cause the problems in the first place, you know?" Daniel said, somewhat taken aback by Todd's attitude.

"Yeah, right, I know," said Todd in a low voice. "That doesn't mean we have to be cheerful."

"Fine." Daniel said. "We're headed for the hideout. Did you bring the cleaning stuff?"

"We left it in the hills on our way over," Craig mumbled.

"Okay, let's go." Daniel took the lead.

As they covered the rough terrain across the hills, Daniel guided Craig and Todd along the most direct route to his hideout. Dactyl joined them, scampering ahead. The landscape around them was typical south-western Saskatchewan – scrubby brush, grassy knolls, stones, and rolling hills. The Bringham farmyard was on the crest of a hill overlooking the Frenchman River Valley. Daniel's hideout was in a natural cave in a coulee between two hills.

Perky gophers darted through the patchy meadow grass to their holes, in the bright morning sunshine. Crows cawed as they winged their way across the valley floor. All around them grasshoppers whirred and tiny flying insects bobbed about their heads. As they scuffed past tallish pale green stalks with long, slender leaves, whiffs of pungent sage wafted up to them.

Craig and Todd said little, and halfway there, they came across the broom, shovel, and several garbage bags the Nelwins had stashed earlier. When they stopped to retrieve them, Daniel unzipped his backpack and reached into the middle section. He handed each of the boys a bottle of water. Gratefully, they accepted and took big swigs. The sun was much higher and hotter now.

"Daniel, can I ask you something?" Craig asked ten-tatively, peering at him out of the corner of his eye.

Daniel waited.

"Do you, uh, do you believe we really went back to dinosaur time?"

Todd shuffled closer to hear the answer.

"What do you think?" Daniel asked.

"Sure felt real," answered Craig.

Beside him, Todd nodded slowly.

"It was scarier than any nightmare I've ever had." Craig offered. "I guess it must have happened."

"I can't think of anything else that makes any sense," admitted Todd.

"There doesn't seem to be any other explanation, does there?" Daniel asked, giving them an opportunity to suggest other reasons, even though he knew it had truly happened.

The boys shuffled uneasily. Almost at the same time, they looked over at the cuts and scrapes on Daniel's arms and legs, easily visible since he wore shorts and a T-shirt. The cuts and scrapes to his body hadn't been there before their trip to prehistoric time.

"The whole episode was as real-life as right now," Daniel said. Then he confessed, "But if I hadn't done it a couple of times before, I wouldn't think it actually happened either."

The boys were silent then, thinking. Craig shivered. Todd's face had a haunted look, as he scuffled off with the tools in his arms. Craig grabbed the rest of the cleaning stuff and followed his brother. Daniel walked along behind them.

By the time they arrived at the hideout, the Nelwins seemed more relaxed in Daniel's company. Dactyl disappeared over a rise as Daniel led the way inside, crawling on his hands and knees. Todd followed. Then Craig brought in the tools.

Most of the larger chunks of debris the Nelwins had strewn about were gathered together into piles, but there were still plenty of bits all over the floor. Broken pieces of rock, bones, parts of a rattlesnake skin, twigs, wrappers from snacks, fossils, and clumps of dirt littered the place from front to back. Sunlight streamed through the hole Daniel had made as a window at the top of the hideout. Off to one side, Daniel's old paleontology research book lay in a heap, tattered, with many of the pages torn out of it.

Daniel set down his backpack and went to retrieve the sections of his almost ruined book. He sat down, heavy-hearted, on his tree stump in the middle of the cave under the skylight opening, sighing as he tried to piece it back together. It was going to take more than glue!

As he worked to reassemble the pages, the Nelwins picked up the bigger chunks of wreckage, tossing them into a garbage bag. Then they stood looking at the piles of stones, arrowheads, animal bones, special rocks, archeological tools, and other items as if they didn't know where to begin.

"Set the rock samples along that wall," Daniel pointed to the back of the hideout. "You can roll up the sleeping bag and set it beside them. The string and twine need to be rewrapped and put into these containers," he nodded towards rusty coffee cans on the floor next to his feet.

"Just leave the piles of stones and fossils where they are. I'll need to bring some new containers."

They'd stomped on the plastic ice cream pails and crushed the coffee tins during their rampage. Daniel also knew they would never be able to sort out the stones and fossil pieces properly. He'd have to do it another time.

A while later, those tasks completed, the brothers began sweeping the floor and gathering the leftovers into the shovel, then dumping it into the garbage bags. Daniel ducked outside to get away from the dust. By now, he'd done the best he could with his book. He'd have to take it home to do any other repairs. He grabbed a side flap to stick it inside his backpack.

Rrrippp. With the flap opened, Daniel's hand stopped in midair. A small pine cone was stuck to the Velcro tab! He dropped the backpack and stepped away. Rooted to the spot, he stared down at the small cone. It must have fallen into his backpack during his last trip into prehistoric time. Maybe it had happened when he and the Nelwins had leapt from the trees after the *Tyrannosaurus rex* had left them for a better meal?

What was he going to do? He was sure the pine cone would work the same way as the piece of redwood bark that had catapulted him and the Nelwins into the past. He couldn't leave it on his backpack. And if he came in contact with it, he knew he'd be hurled back into the past again as quick as a bee sting. Sure, he could probably drop the cone to return to his current life, but would he be lucky enough to escape being seriously injured or eaten before he could come back?

He shuddered just thinking about the final thing he'd experienced the time before. He'd nearly lost his life — narrowly escaping a small, fast, meat-eating theropod dinosaur with its deadly sickle-like claw on each foot, which had attacked just before he'd suddenly returned to the present.

What if he removed the cone with a stick or something? But even if he unstuck it from his backpack, where would he keep it? He needed somewhere safe so that no one else would be exposed to it. He recalled again how the Nelwins had intruded into his special place and discovered it. He didn't want anything like that to happen again. But thinking about the Nelwins brought him back to the present. They must almost be finished cleaning. He had to do something with the cone before they came out.

Taking a deep breath, Daniel seized a branch from near the entranceway of his hideout — one he figured would do the job properly. Quickly, he stripped the branch of dead leaves and twigs. Then he took another gulp of air. Reaching out with the stick, he stood for a few moments unsure if he was about to disappear. He held his breath as he gathered his courage. Then, quickly, he jabbed at the cone with the tip of his stick. Nothing happened. He drew back.

Okay, he had to be directly touching it before anything could happen. He nudged at it again. The Velcro on the backpack held the cone fast against his soft proddings. He stabbed a third time, using more force.

All at once it let go and flipped into the air. Daniel watched the cone rise as if in slow motion. It did a slow twirl and landed nearly touching his left foot. He jumped back with a little yelp.

Just then, Craig thrust his head outside the hideout. He stopped short, causing Todd to holler at him from behind. Craig stared at Daniel, taking in the situation. He cowered back. Todd squeezed out past him and came to an abrupt halt.

Daniel stood still, not daring to move. "Don't touch it!" he yelled.

"Is that from dinosaur time?" Todd asked in a low, scared voice.

Daniel nodded.

Craig shuddered. "Keep it away from me!"

"You bet I will," said Daniel. "I don't want anyone to touch it. I just don't know what to do about it yet!"

"Where did it come from?" Craig's voice quavered.

Daniel explained his suspicions. Todd and Craig sidled away from the cone and moved behind Daniel.

"How about burying it?" Todd asked.

"But what if someone or some animal accidentally uncovered it?" Daniel asked.

"Bury it really deep," suggested Craig.

"I wouldn't trust that! We could get a big rain and then wind could erode the dirt away!" Daniel said. "That's how many fossils came to be discovered."

"How about hiding it in there?" Craig pointed to

Daniel's hideout. "At least the weather wouldn't get directly at it."

Daniel thought about it for a few moments, eyeing the Nelwins suspiciously.

Todd spoke up. "We wouldn't go looking for it. Promise!"

Craig shook his head. "No way. We don't want to be anywhere near it again!"

"You'll be the only one who knows where it is," said Todd.

"We won't ever come back to your hideout again, either," Craig promised.

"That's right!" Todd agreed.

"Okay," Daniel decided reluctantly. "Are you finished in there?"

"Yes," said Todd.

"Get your stuff, and you can go back to the farm, while I figure out how to do this," Daniel directed them. "Find my dad, and he'll tell you what needs doing next."

The brothers scrambled back into the hideout and within moments had shoved out the tools and bags of garbage. Outside, they gathered everything into their arms and left. With barely a backward glance, they lit across the hills and soon disappeared from sight. They didn't even wait to see what Daniel would do next.

Daniel's mind was on his precarious task. Would he be able to hide the cone safely without being flung back in time?

CHAPTER THREE

Daniel stood rooted to the spot for a few more minutes. How was he going to move the cone? Obviously, using a stick wasn't reliable. Then he remembered an old garden trowel he had in his hideout. At least, he hoped it was still there. Carefully, he stepped around the pine cone and crawled into the dark recesses of his cave.

Once he located the trowel, he scanned the walls. He found the perfect spot – a small crevice about halfway down the east wall that he could dig a little deeper. He worked away at it, forming a hole. Once this was accomplished, he crawled back outside.

Cautiously, he edged the trowel under the dangerous cone until it rested in the middle. Daniel wiped away the sweat that was forming on his brow – knowing it wasn't from the heat of the sun's sharp rays. Grasping the trowel handle with two hands, he softly trod over to the hideout doorway. Gently, he pushed the trowel inside and set it down beside the door, making sure the cone was stable. He crawled inside, and slowly picked it up again.

As he made his way to the freshly dug crevice, he held his breath. With great care, he tipped the trowel and let the pine cone slide into the opening, pushing it firmly into place. Then he found a stone and plugged the hole, making sure his fingers didn't touch the cone. Next, he patted moist dirt from the floor over the hole, using the trowel to smooth the wall until no seams showed.

Relieved, Daniel plopped himself down on his tree stump, and let the trowel slide from his hand. He gave a huge sigh and wiped the sweat from his forehead. The pine cone was safely hidden for the time being. Once the dirt dried, no one would see anything unusual.

Except *he'd* know where it was. Could he leave it there? Or would he be tempted to make use of it?

Imagine discovering new information and being able to verify some of the things the scientists debated? One thing he could do right now was tell them about the colours of the various creatures. But he couldn't prove it.

Suddenly, a thought struck Daniel. What if he were to go back in time on purpose? He could make sure he was prepared with the proper equipment. Why not make use of the cone? A tremor of fear ran up his spine. No, he couldn't do it! What if a carnivore dinosaur actually succeeded in attacking him? No one would know where he was and no one would be able to help him! His parents would never know what had happened to him.

He shook his head and got up. It was time to get back to the farm and see how things were going. He hadn't heard any whistling, but then he wasn't outside where he could listen for it either. He gave one last look at the hiding spot and left. Dactyl joined him moments later.

Hustling home, Daniel found ideas popping through his mind like kernels in a hot-air popcorn maker. If he *did* go back to prehistoric time, a camera would be great and maybe he could bring back samples of plants. Then he jerked his thoughts back to the present. The journey would simply be too dangerous!

When he reached the yard, Dactyl wandered off and Daniel made his way to the tourist campsite. Craig and Todd ignored him when he arrived. Craig concentrated on applying a layer of stain over the exterior outhouse walls that he'd covered with spray-painted swear words a couple of nights before. Todd kept himself busy sanding the tops of the picnic tables. He'd etched his initials into them with his pocket knife. Daniel saw that one of them had also pounded out the dints in the forty-five-gallon water barrel that they had dumped Daniel into and then rolled down the hill.

"Hello, Daniel," said Dad, appearing from behind the stack of firewood with Mr. Lindstrom just behind him. "How's it going?"

"Great." Daniel glanced over at the Nelwins. "Should I go help them?"

Both men shook their heads in unison.

Dad said, "They have to learn the full value of consequences." Then he asked how the Nelwins did at the barn.

"Okay," answered Daniel. "So, what would you like me to do?"

"Would you mind checking the horses?" Dad asked.

Mr. Lindstrom agreed. "See how they're doing for water and such, seeing as how this is their first day here."

"You bet," said Daniel, happy to have a responsible job to do, although he doubted it was as important as Dad and Mr. Lindstrom made it out to be. They were probably trying to spare his feelings, because they figured he couldn't do much strenuous physical work. Still, it kept him occupied.

He puttered about with his dad and Mr. Lindstrom, doing the less demanding chores, readying the campsite for all the guests, until Jed's two youngest sisters called them for lunch. When they arrived back in the yard, Dad and Mr. Lindstrom hopped out of the jeep and went straight into the outdoor kitchen to wash up. But when Daniel poked his head in, his Mom asked him to wash Cheryl outside.

"The rest of you can wash out there too." She threw him a couple of older towels.

Daniel headed to the trough and water pump with Cheryl chattering and squirming, as she tried to get down to pet Dactyl, who had just arrived. The rest of the group, including Jed's sisters and the Nelwins, straggled behind.

He set Cheryl down at the low wooden trough, which normally was used for watering the livestock. She splashed her hands into the water, laughing as she got herself wet. Daniel primed the pump and caught fresh water in a basin. He returned it to its wooden stand and washed his hands. Then he propelled Cheryl over and washed hers. By the time their hands were dry, Craig and Todd had joined them. Wordlessly, the brothers washed up.

"I don't know about you, but I'm hungry," Daniel said to break the silence.

"Suppose so," Todd grunted, bending to plunge his hands under the stream of water that Craig pumped.

Craig caught the last of the water with his hands and gave a quick rinse. Lindsay and her sisters strode up then and Craig pumped the water for them with one hand.

"Thanks," Lindsay said, seeming surprised at Craig's helpfulness. Then she reached for Cheryl. "Can I take her now?"

"Sure." Daniel handed her over. Cheryl did one of her koala bear hugs around Lindsay and they trotted off with Leanne and Lucy beside them, stopping to pick wild-flowers to tuck in their hair.

Hurrying to the camp kitchen, Daniel found Craig and Todd loitering outside under the tree with the swing on it. From inside the building, they could hear the scraping of benches and clatter of utensils, along with the chattering of several voices.

"Come on," he called, quickening his pace. "The others are already eating."

Timidly, Craig and Todd followed Daniel inside.

"You can sit right over here, boys," Mom indicated a bench behind the table where the three of them would fit.

She passed them glasses filled with ice cubes and juice, and the others began handing dishes of food to them. Daniel filled his plate with ham and cheese sandwiches, some dill pickles, and a mound of potato salad. Craig heaped on extra potato salad. Todd stacked his plate full of sandwiches, and then he looked guiltily around, because he'd almost decimated them all.

"Eat hearty," said Dad. "I know there are plenty more!"

After they'd eaten, the Nelwins hung about under the trees, waiting for Dad and Doug Lindstrom to finish gathering some tools they needed. Mr. Pederson appeared unexpectedly in the yard, and walked straight over to Daniel.

"How's it going, lad?" he asked cheerfully.

"Great! How about with you at the dig?"

"Couldn't be better," he said. His face crinkled with a smile.

"You've found something?" Daniel whispered.

"We'll see," he said, his eyes lit with excitement. Then he turned serious. "I need to talk to you about the quarry. I think we're soon going to need quite a bit more overburden removed."

"Maybe I could come out and dig tomorrow morning?" Daniel suggested.

"You need to mend, lad." Pederson shook his head.

"But I'm feeling fine now!" he protested.

"And we need you for the tours," Pederson said, calming Daniel down. "You're the best we have! Besides, there'll be plenty more digging later on."

Resigning himself to the fact that he wouldn't be able to do any heavy work for a few days, Daniel guessed what Pederson was going to recommend.

"This might be the time to try Craig and Todd," Pederson suggested. They'd been asked the day before, and they were enthusiastic.

Daniel started to protest. Even though he'd agreed to the suggestion at first, he wasn't so sure he wanted them on-site after all. He still didn't trust them after their attacks on him over the last couple of days. Had they learned their lesson? Even if they had, could they change their behaviour that fast? Yet they had worked hard and quickly so far this morning. Maybe he should give them a chance.

Pederson gave Daniel's shoulder a squeeze, sensing his doubts. "Let's see how they do. If they don't work out, well, there's nothing lost."

"Sure." Daniel cracked a smile. "I guess we can use all the help we can get." There was plenty of work to do if they were going to uncover more sections of the fossils that they'd already found before fall came.

"That's the spirit, lad," Pederson patted Daniel's arm. "You can just sit back and watch the rest of us work and enjoy the results – looks like there may be plenty."

Pederson walked over and acknowledged the Nelwins, who were sitting morosely at the picnic table.

"Are you boys ready to do some volunteer work out at the excavation site later today?"

Instantly, their manner changed and their faces lit up with smiles.

"Yeah." Todd's eyes brightened.

Craig looked at Mr. Pederson happily. "Sure!"

Pederson explained. "It's not the greatest job. It's only digging, mind, but it needs to be done so that we can get to the good stuff, but it will give you a chance to see what's going on."

"We'll be there!"

"I'll expect you later this afternoon, then, as soon as you've completed your work for Mr. Bringham. Daniel will bring you out."

"Okay!" Todd said with a smile.

"Yes, sir!" Craig said with real enthusiasm.

Pederson nodded to the Nelwins. Then he headed into the outdoor kitchen for a quick bite of lunch. The Nelwins spoke excitedly to one another in low voices. Daniel couldn't make out what they were saying, but somehow he felt okay about Mr. Pederson giving the Nelwins an opportunity to work on the excavation and be part of the group excitement.

A sudden roaring of an engine and grinding of gears turned Daniel's attention towards the road. He watched as a creaky '78 Mazda pickup truck with a well-used topper over the box turned into their driveway. Daniel couldn't tell at first if it was a man or a woman driving, but whoever it was, that person was alone. The truck lurched to a stop a few yards from him; its wheel wells rusted out and nothing much left of the fenders.

The driver's side door opened. First a metal cane appeared, and then a couple of long, stocky legs in baggy sweatpants. Finally, a tall older woman wearing a Tilley hat squashed onto her head emerged.

"Dr. Roost!" Daniel called as he hurried to her truck. Within moments, she was surrounded by everyone in the yard.

"Hello all," Mildred Roost pushed her hat higher onto her forehead. "Came to see your new digs." She laughed at her own pun, as she swept her cane from right to left, taking in people scattered throughout the property, doing various activities. "Looks like you're right busy."

After the introductions were made, everyone tried to speak at once, but Mom broke through. "Can we offer you a drink or something to eat?"

"A cold drink might be a good idea," she said. "Could use a speck of shade too," she added.

As she headed towards the picnic table under the nearby tree, Daniel and Dad followed her with Cheryl in tow. The Lindstroms and Nelwins hung back, making small talk. A moment later, Ole Pederson emerged from the outdoor kitchen.

"Mildred," Mr. Pederson said, going over to shake her hand. His eyes lit up with pleasure. "How splendid to see you!"

Mom arrived with a glass of iced tea for Mildred Roost, setting a piece of lemon pie in front of her.

"Can we do anything else for you?" asked Dad.

"This looks just fine!" said Dr. Roost, digging her fork into the meringue.

"Are you here for a while? Do you need a place to stay?" Daniel asked, excited that she had come to see them.

"Thought I'd stop for bit," she answered, taking a sip of iced tea and sighing in contentment. "All I need is a place to squat."

"We have a spare room in the house," Mom offered. "It's a little small, but the bed is comfy."

Daniel could see his dad was thinking about the guesthouse at the other end of the caragana hedge, but it wasn't quite finished yet. There were a few more things they wanted to do inside and out to make it more comfortable.

"Sounds a little too fancy for me. I have my own roof." She pointed to the back of her truck. "I just need somewhere to park it," Dr. Roost declared.

"The campsite is just down there." Daniel pointed down the valley.

"There are still a couple of places," Dad said.

Mildred tilted her head as if sizing up the suggestions, then she looked around the farmyard.

"I could park in the yard – maybe over behind that stand of trees. Hope that's all right with you?"

Her overbearing manner left little room for discussion, but Daniel's parents didn't seem to mind.

"That would leave your campsite for more guests. I'm sure you're going to be full up soon." She jerked her head towards the driveway as two more vehicles pulled into the yard.

"Sure thing," said Dad, laughing.

They watched Lucy and Jed go over to greet the newcomers. Excusing herself, Mom picked up Cheryl and went back to the kitchen, followed by Greta Lindstrom, Lindsay, and Leanne. Moments later, Dad and Doug Lindstrom had the Nelwins in the back of the jeep and they headed back down to the campsite. Daniel hovered beside Mr. Pederson.

"So this is where you've created all the excitement." Mildred Roost pushed her hat up even farther on her forehead and peered at Pederson.

"What really brings you here?" Pederson asked.

"You," she said simply. "I came to see what you've been up to. Uncover anything good lately?"

Pederson hesitated, and then answered with a dismissing shrug of his shoulders. "Nothing much for certain."

"You always did hedge about when you were onto something good," she said, chuckling. Her brown eyes shone excitedly from her wizened face. "Must be something spectacular."

Pederson couldn't stop a crack of a smile. "We'll see."

She fixed piercing eyes on him, but he said no more.

As the two continued their conversation, Daniel felt like an intruder. "Well, I'm off," he said, finally finding an opening in their conversation.

"See you later, lad," Mr. Pederson said distractedly.

Daniel would catch up on their news later. He had other thoughts whirring around in his mind – like planning his trip to the prehistoric world. Maybe the rest of the day wouldn't be too busy. But just as Daniel finished that thought, three more vehicles pulled into the yard, one after another. He walked over to show them where to park. Lucy appeared with papers in hand.

For the rest of the afternoon, Daniel, Jed, and Lucy were kept busy sorting the tourists and guiding them on the hiking trails or to the quarry, and taking them to the campsite. Jed and Lucy mostly did the quarry and hiking tours, and Daniel did the horse trails, which he found a little easier on his bruised body. Most people decided to spend the night. Dad and Doug Lindstrom assisted them in choosing spots and setting up their camping gear. In between times, the men worked on finishing the exterior of the guesthouse. Mildred Roost had gone to the quarry with Ole Pederson some time earlier, both of them chatting without any indication of stopping soon.

Daniel guided the Nelwins to help Mr. Pederson about mid-afternoon. Dactyl seemed content to stay in the farmyard. As the trio left sight of the farm buildings, Daniel stopped and pointed to the hills across the valley where different coloured layers of earth were evident.

"Do you see those striation lines?" Todd and Craig nodded.

"Those are sedimentary layers indicating different geological formations. The further you go down, the older they are. The one that's almost black – about two-thirds of the way down the valley – is a coal seam that contains the K-T boundary. In it is a white, pasty clay layer that has all the geochemical signatures of meteor impact. That layer separates the Cretaceous and Tertiary Periods – the extinction of the dinosaur world."

"Amazing that we can actually see where the changes happened," said Craig.

"Yeah, I never thought about what was below us before," said Todd.

Then Craig, with a curious expression, asked, "Is that about where we were when we went back in time?"

"Yes," said Daniel, studying the hillsides. "It's hard to tell exactly where, because we're talking about millions of years in time."

"Wow." Todd seemed mesmerized by the implications.

"Weird how you can actually see the past in the present," said Craig.

"Wait until we get to the quarry," Daniel said. "You'll even see more things like that. We have some evidence of garfish skeletons."

"But those are fish from now, aren't they?" asked Todd.

Daniel said, "You're right. They do live now in the southern United States and in South America, but they've existed for millions of years. They look very much the same today, except they are quite a bit smaller. They somehow made it through all the extinctions with many of the other creatures."

"I thought everything went extinct with the dinosaurs," said Craig.

"Not all creatures," Daniel said. "Some adapted."

"You mean everything didn't just die off right when the meteor struck?" Todd asked in amazement.

"No, the extinction of some creatures took many thousands and millions of years, and some of them evolved over time," Daniel explained.

"Aren't birds supposed to be related to the dinosaurs?" asked Craig.

Daniel turned to him in surprise. "How do you know that?"

"It just makes sense because of the way they both walk." Craig blushed when Daniel continued to stare at him. "I was looking through your dinosaur book," he admitted.

Daniel grinned. Craig was getting hooked on paleontology!

As Todd and Craig discussed the point, Daniel's mind drifted off again to all the layers of creatures that had lived at various prehistoric times several metres beneath them – in an alien world so many fathomless years in the past.

He pictured the prehistoric shorebirds they'd seen, wondering exactly what type of insects they ate. Were any of those insects poisonous? And what about the herbivores, would they totally ignore humans? He sure would like to go back and investigate these things in more detail. A sudden trembling swept through him at the thought of the danger he would be in and he quickly brushed the thought away.

They reached the last hilltop and began their descent into the quarry. Daniel couldn't see any sign of Mr. Pederson or Mildred Roost. Where had they gone?

All at once, he spied Pederson lying on the ground at the edge of a narrow ledge, slightly hidden from view by an overhang. He must have found something! Daniel whistled their special code, but there was no response. He gave another piercing whistle. Nothing happened.

Daniel realized that Mr. Pederson was lying on his back, an unusual position when one was looking for fossils. And he wasn't moving at all! Not even a finger, nor could Daniel detect any rise and fall of his chest! Daniel didn't want to alarm the others, but what if something had happened to Mr. Pederson? And where was Dr. Roost?

Daniel hollered as loud as he could, yet held back his fear. "Mr. Pederson!" No answer. "Mr. Pederson!"

Again, there was no response. "Dr. Roost!" he hollered. "Mr. Pederson!"

Maybe he'd had a heart attack! Daniel gathered speed as he watched the prone body on the ledge below him. The others followed behind, seeming to sense something exciting, but not realizing Daniel's fear.

Stumbling down the steep incline, Daniel rounded a curve and ran as fast as he could towards Mr. Pederson's prone body.

CHAPTER FOUR

As Daniel crunched his way over the cleared terrain of the excavation site, he kicked up clouds of dust. Breathing hard, he kept his eye on Mr. Pederson, still calling as he ran.

"Mr. Pederson! Mr. Pederson!"

There was no movement. Daniel leapt down to the ledge where Mr. Pederson's inert body lay, and shouted again as he plopped down beside him.

Suddenly, Mr. Pederson sat up and looked at Daniel with a surprised expression on his face.

"What's wrong, Daniel?" He rose to his feet.

"Geez, Mr. Pederson, you scared me!"

"I scared *you*? You scared the living daylights out of me by almost jumping on top of me," Mr. Pederson complained.

"I thought you were dead or something. You weren't moving." Daniel wiped the sweat out of his eyes. His heart thumped against his chest.

"Of course not, I was resting," the old man said, rubbing his eyes.

"Couldn't you hear me calling?" asked Daniel.

Pederson stared at Daniel. "I was underneath the overhang, out of the sun. I couldn't hear anything. It was so peaceful and quiet. And if you must know, I was having a rather pleasant dream."

The Nelwins had arrived on the hill directly above them. Daniel waved to them. He tried to calm himself, relieved that Mr. Pederson was all right.

"But where's Dr. Roost?"

Pederson waved his arm. "Off exploring somewhere. Last time I saw her, she was heading over that rise." He pointed to a distant hill.

The Nelwins joined them then and Pederson gave them a genial welcome.

"Until I explain everything to you, please stay outside the tied-off areas," he said, rising to his feet and brushing dust off his pants. "You'll see how tiny some of our discoveries are in a moment, and one footstep can make all the difference in destroying some prime finds."

He guided them to a particularly rocky plateau nearby. "This is what we call a microsite and this is what we find here."

In less than a minute, Mr. Pederson picked up several kinds of specimens, so small that they all fit into the palm of one hand. He pointed to each of them. "Small mammal teeth, ear bones, several leaf fossils and plant seeds, bits of turtle shell, crocodile armour, salamanders, tiny vertebrae from garfish, and *Triceratops* teeth."

"Sheesh!" Craig bent over for a closer inspection. "You can tell what all of these are?"

"Yes, lad!" Pederson said with confidence. "Comes from years of practice."

Todd crowded in for a closer look. "I can see why you don't want us stepping all over the place!" he said.

Pederson nodded.

"Sir, how do you know where to look for these kinds of areas, and the bigger fossils too?" asked Craig.

"We go on 'prospecting' tours," Pederson explained. "We usually do exploratory trips through the hills in teams of a couple of people so we don't miss any spots."

"But how can you tell dinosaur bones from rocks?"

Pederson laughed. "Actually we look for shapes, textures, and things that *don't* look like stone. With practice you get an eye for it, don't you Daniel?"

"That's right, sir!" Daniel said. He'd been doing it as long as he could remember. "And by taste!"

Daniel picked up a small stone and then a piece of fossilized bone from Mr. Pederson's hand. He demonstrated the difference between them by touching the stone to his tongue.

"See, the stone is solid in the centre and doesn't stick, but…" he removed the stone from the edge of his tongue and replaced it with the fossil, which stuck fast. He tried to explain. "The bone thiks to ur tung."

He removed the fossil. "Bones are porous, that's why it sticks."

"Cool," said Craig. "Would we be able to go prospecting sometime?"

"We won't be doing anything like that for quite a while. We have plenty to excavate right here," Pederson answered. "Although I suppose it's something special we could consider offering to the public too. I'm not sure we could do it this year."

Then he saw the disappointed look on the boys' faces. "We're rather booked up with tours, especially for the rest of the summer, but maybe after that we could work it in somehow, if you're still keen."

Craig's eyes shone with interest. Todd shrugged his shoulders, as if it didn't matter to him one way or the other.

"It would be cool to discover something!" Craig said. "Would it be named after us?"

"Could be." Pederson laughed. "And now for the macrosite where all the big fossils are located." He turned to Daniel, his eyes twinkling in excitement. "You'll want to take a look at this too. I uncovered something new today."

Pederson led them over to his excavation area first, where several ribs poked out of the ground. As he explained how he had uncovered them, Daniel looked closer. There were several more bones exposed, over to the right of the ones found earlier. They were inverted and not in line with the rest.

"This skeleton is disarticulated, which in scientific terms means the bones are scattered," explained Pederson. "The skeleton is in a former riverbed and the current has washed it downstream, which caused it to come apart."

He led them over to Daniel's section.

"This lad here," he patted Daniel's shoulder, "uncovered these teeth, which we know are from a herbivore. These are important, because they are probably part of the skeleton from over there and that's what helps us identify it."

"Why do you think that?" asked Craig.

Pederson explained. "As the carcass of any animal rots, the teeth often come apart from the jaws. With the water velocity of the river 65 million years ago, these teeth were probably separated from the body."

As Craig and Todd stood mesmerized, Daniel beamed with pride at his findings. He remembered how thrilled he'd been discovering pieces from a much larger creature.

Pederson continued. "All we can do is hope that most of the skeleton is here in the vicinity to help us identify it more accurately."

"Do you have enough yet to know what this one is?" Craig asked.

"Just those pieces are not enough to go on." Then, with a gleam in his eyes, Pederson pulled a tarp off a section and stepped back to reveal a much larger bone partially protruding from the ground. "But this is what I found so far today."

Daniel moved closer and stared. A partial skull! Without thinking about the others possibly following him and the restrictions they had for staying behind the ropes, he went closer to examine it. Sinking to his knees, he examined the skull more closely. He touched the dark brown contours, running his hands over the huge, rough, sunken eye sockets. If it was what he thought it was, this would be the first one found in Saskatchewan.

"*Stygimoloch*. Maybe," Pederson said, hardly able to contain himself.

Daniel whooped! His guess had been right. "Wow! Really?"

Pederson nodded. "I'm reasonably sure."

"Does Dr. Roost know?" Daniel asked, wondering about her reaction.

"No, lad, I wanted you to see it first. I wouldn't let her peek."

Daniel felt his body swell with pride. Mr. Pederson was treating him like an equal, a colleague! Daniel felt a huge grin spread across his face.

Pederson turned to include the Nelwins. "We always suspected that *Stygimoloch* would have been in this area too, but so far they've only been found across the border in Montana and in Wyoming. If this turns out be one, it will prove they lived here too."

The Nelwins seemed entranced as Pederson explained that the creatures were unusual looking, with bony spikes and bumps on their skulls. "We'll have to find more of the skeleton, and do some research, examinations, and comparisons to be certain if this is really one."

Then Pederson turned to them and warned, "You're the first ones to hear about this, so you'll need to keep it a secret for the time being. Can you do that?"

Todd and Craig nodded in agreement.

"When will it become public knowledge?" asked Craig.

"Depends on how much of the skeleton we find and what we can prove once it's excavated."

"How long will that take?" Todd asked.

"Again, that will depend on what we find and how difficult it is to extract – whether there's a great deal of rock and topsoil, and whether it's spread over a wide area or not. We could have it out as early as the end of this summer, which is what I hope, but it most likely will take longer. Even several years."

"So we have to keep it secret for a long time?" Craig asked.

"That's one of the hardest parts about paleontology – keeping the information from the public until we know for certain," Daniel said, knowing from experience.

His excitement at finding fossils always took over his reasoning, and he wanted to broadcast it to everyone right away. Already, Daniel could hardly wait to tell Jed and Lucy, and the rest of their families, what they had found. But that would have to wait until they had more evidence. Several of the Lindstrom family members had a difficult time keeping secrets, Jed included. And the *Stygimoloch* was an important find that would bring lots more tourists to their site. No point in letting the immediate group know too far ahead in case they slipped with the information when visitors came. They didn't want anyone leaking information that might be wrong.

"We can discuss it amongst ourselves here and let the rest of our group know back at the house once we have verified it," Pederson confirmed.

Staying on their farm depended on the success of their dinosaur tourist camp and the excavation site operation. If they didn't make a go of it, Daniel knew they'd have to leave and he would be far removed from the paleontology that he loved. This discovery was an exciting bonus to their findings and would be sure to keep them on the farm.

And all at once, Daniel realized how much he wanted to return to the prehistoric past. Going there again would be an exceptional opportunity to explore, and maybe he'd even see a live *Stygimoloch*. He didn't recall coming across any of them when he'd accidentally travelled back before. But then he'd been too intent on surviving and hadn't stuck around to look for much of anything. Now his thoughts had turned to the possibility of going on a deliberate exploration of the world of dinosaurs. He had an almost sure way of going and coming back. All he had to do was plan it properly.

Daniel hardly listened as Pederson said, "Finding something interesting is one thing, but getting it out is another." He indicated the shovels and pointed to the lofty hill.

"Why is it done like that?" asked Craig, staring at the wide, square levels cut progressively into the hillside like a huge set of stairs. Each step was about a metre square and about thirty centimetres high.

"It keeps the wall solid as we excavate," Pederson said. "If we had a sheer face, there would probably be some slippage and breaking off, which would bury what we've already uncovered in the fossil bed below. This way, we can contain it and also have a more convenient way of getting up and down."

Mr. Pederson said. "Most paleontological work is pure hard digging. You only get to work around actual fossils with the smaller tools about one-third of the time." He turned to Craig and Todd. "So, boys, what do you think so far?"

Todd's enthusiasm seemed to diminish with the mention of all the digging, but Craig seemed keen. "Where do you want us to start?"

As Mr. Pederson directed the Nelwins' digging, Daniel sidled off with a hasty wave goodbye. He quickened his steps across the pasture, almost forgetting how tired and sore his legs were from all the walking he'd done that day. He'd suddenly remembered that he hadn't checked his computer at all that day. He and Mr. Pederson were expecting some e-mailed photographs of Roxanne, the *Edmontosaurus* that Mr. Pederson had found and they had excavated together.

Members of the staff at the Royal Saskatchewan Museum field station in Eastend were preparing the skeleton, under the direction of Tim Tokaryk, the head paleontologist there. Some breakage on the left hindquarter had been evident, which might help explain why Roxanne had died.

His legs ached as he mounted the stairs to his bedroom. When he looked in the mirror, he could see the sweat stains and the streaks of dirt on his face and neck. Time for another shower! Better yet, a long soak in the tub was what he needed. But that would have to wait. He turned on his computer, started his e-mail account, and searched for one from the Royal Saskatchewan Museum.

There it was! Quickly, he opened it. The museum staff had sent three photographs of the left hindquarter breakages of the *Edmontosaurus* skeleton from different angles and distances. There was also one of Roxanne's skull, which showed a fracture, and another showing where she had suffered a break in one of her forearms. He studied the photographs for a few moments.

They'd sent an explanation that suggested that the leg and hip bone breakages suffered by the *Edmontosaurus* probably were serious enough to cause her to starve to death. None of the fractures had healed at the time of her death, according to their findings. This coupled with the discovery of a nest with fully developed embryos and some newly hatched babies, suggested that they had all died about the same time.

Daniel felt sadness welling up inside him. Because the mother hadn't been able to fend for herself and feed her young, they'd all died. He thought of an injured female *Edmontosaurus* that he'd come across on his last trip back to prehistoric time. This must be the same one! Wait until he told Mr. Pederson. If only he could prove it.

The more he thought about confirming his observations, the more he realized how important it would be if he could actually go back and do some other investigations as well. One thing he'd have to take was some kind of marker system, so he'd be able to return to the same spot.

Wait! What was he thinking? It wasn't safe to go! But a quick trip couldn't be that bad, could it? The opportunity was there with the pine cone. He could go back one last time. He wrestled with the idea, his thoughts whirring like a hamster racing on a treadmill. He made a decision, and then changed his mind again. Should he really go back in time? He looked again at Roxanne's skeleton images. He had to know more.

In that moment, Daniel made the firm decision to go back to the past. He'd photograph the *Edmontosaurus* family! He'd gather everything he needed over the next few days, and when there was a lull with the tourists, he'd go. With Dr. Roost here, Mr. Pederson would be occupied and not notice his actions quite so much.

He started a new Word file and began a list of what he'd need to take. Camera, flashlight, compass, water, food –

how much and what should he take? He'd leave that for the moment. A hat, backpack, good running shoes, bug spray, suntan lotion, a dinosaur research book, and his Swiss Army knife sounded like a good start. He'd add more to the list later, although he probably didn't need to take much – he was only going to be gone several minutes.

He added a few more things – waterproof matches, a notebook, pens, pencils, tape measure, extra batteries for the flashlight, adhesive tape, and a whistle. He didn't want to rely on whistling with his fingers, if he were in danger. He might not be loud enough to scare away any of the prehistoric creatures.

His list was getting long, and he hadn't even written down the food and clothing he'd need, nor any of the tools. Besides, why was he planning to take so much stuff, if he was only going to be gone a short time? Might as well be prepared, he decided. He didn't even want to think yet about how he'd survive against any dinosaur attacks. He'd figure that out later.

Daniel was so preoccupied with his plans that he didn't even notice Pederson and Dr. Roost return from the dig and slip out of the yard a while later. He did his chores with the Nelwins mechanically and ate his supper in a haze, going through the usual motions for the rest of the evening. His mind was a kaleidoscope of ideas that kept him tuned out from the rest of his surroundings.

Before bed, Daniel ran a nice, full, hot tub of water, adding some Epsom salts. He sank gratefully into the soothing bath, staying there until the skin on his fingers shrivelled and the water cooled. Then he dressed in his pyjamas and crawled into bed, pulling a sheet around himself. The overhead fan whirled a slight breeze over him from the window. The evening was hot and the sun was just setting. He didn't care. He'd already been up for too many busy hours. Plans for going back in time spun through his mind. But exhaustion finally overtook him, and moments later he slipped into sleep.

CHAPTER FIVE

By the time Daniel dressed and made it down-stairs the next morning, Ole Pederson was there again, sipping coffee at the kitchen table. He and Dad were going over the list of visitors for the day. Apparently Dr. Roost had already been and gone from the house.

The Nelwins arrived at the door a few minutes later, knocking timidly. They shuffled in when Mom invited them to join the family for breakfast and sat self-consciously at the table, but soon relaxed when everyone began eating. Daniel noticed that the Nelwins seemed more polite and comfortable when his mom spoke to them. He remembered hearing that they had lost their mother several years before — it must be hard for them.

Today it was bacon and eggs for breakfast and this time the Nelwins didn't wait to be offered seconds. They'd probably had to do their chores for their dad before they came over.

Todd ate with his head down, not saying a word, and Cheryl watched him, fascinated. Finally he noticed and looked up. Cheryl laughed and plunked a crust from her toast on his plate. For a moment, Todd looked flustered, then he broke into a grin and ate the toast. Daniel saw his mom and dad exchange a small smile.

"Ed, I think we're going to need some walkie-talkies to communicate between the dig and the house," Mr. Pederson suggested with an expressionless face. "Whistling doesn't always work, as Daniel and I found out yesterday."

Daniel sat stone-faced. He hadn't mentioned the scare Mr. Pederson had given him the previous afternoon. Daniel was grateful that the Nelwins had kept quiet too.

"Being able to let Mr. Pederson know we're coming ahead of time would be helpful, Dad."

"Well, how about I give you my cellphone to use at the site, Ole? Doug and I will share his until we have a chance to shop for some walkie-talkies."

"I'd rather not use one of those contraptions," said Mr. Pederson.

Mom interrupted with another suggestion. "I think the kids are getting worn out from making so many trips to the quarry anyway. Could we send them with slightly larger groups at more definite times?"

"That's an excellent idea!" Mr. Pederson said. "Then we wouldn't need a communication system to alert me when to expect them. I'd know beforehand."

Dad agreed. "I don't know why we didn't think about that before."

"Also, I'd get a little more work done," Ole Pederson added. "I haven't had a chance to tell you what I uncovered yesterday." An expression of pure pleasure spread across his face as he explained about the possible *Stygimoloch*.

Everyone clapped and cheered at the news. Even Cheryl joined in laughing and clapping, wanting to be part of the group, but not understanding what the commotion was all about.

"I'm going to keep the skull hidden under a tarp for now, and continue to leave it out of the tour until we do more excavating. I'd like to identify it officially. Do you think we could keep it quiet? Just between us all here in the house?" Mr. Pederson eyed those around the table.

Everyone agreed. They all knew the Lindstrom family's problem with secrets.

"I have some news too," Daniel said. He told them about the photographs on his computer.

Pederson shoved back his chair and stood up. "Let's go take a look, lad!"

Daniel and Ole Pederson made it up to his room in record time with the others trailing behind. After he turned on his computer, they stayed glued to it for some time, examining the photos of Roxanne. Dad, Mom, and Cheryl soon lost interest and left. The Nelwins went to start the barn chores, although Craig lingered longer than Todd.

After everyone else had left, Daniel explained his theories to Ole Pederson. "I think it's probably the same dinosaur that I saw when the Nelwins and I were back in time."

"You may be right, lad, but we'll never know for sure."

Daniel just about blurted out his plan of returning. Instead, he held his tongue. Mr. Pederson wouldn't let him go, if he knew.

Mr. Pederson returned downstairs, while Daniel readied himself for the day, making his bed and tidying his room. The sound of crunching gravel under his window indicated the Lindstroms had arrived, and he hadn't even done the milking yet. He hurried from his room.

Outside he found Mildred Roost ready with all her gear strapped around her, making her look like a linebacker prepared to tackle. An old canvas bag sat hunched on her back and a worn leather carpenter's belt around her waist stowed all her picks and chisels. As usual, her Tilley hat sat slightly off-kilter towards the back of her head. She propelled herself across the yard towards the garden while she waited for Mr. Pederson to join her. Poking here and there with the tip of her cane, she examined the produce, checking for tomatoes under the leaves and tapping the cornstalks.

Laughing at her investigative style, Daniel continued to the barn, but when she caught sight of him, she called him over.

"Young man, I hear you've been having some interesting adventures."

Daniel eyed her suspiciously. What was she referring to?

"I guess so," he answered evasively.

She leaned closer to him. "You can tell me all about the prehistoric trips." She lowered her voice almost to a whisper.

"Did Mr. Pederson...?"

"Yes, he told me. He was worried about you," she said. "I'd like to hear about it."

Reluctantly, Daniel gave her a brief synopsis of his encounters, making sure no one else overheard them.

Mildred Roost glowed with interest. "We'll have to have further conversations," she said. "I'd like to hear more of the details."

"I could show you the sketches I made sometime," Daniel offered.

Seeing as how she hadn't sloughed his stories off as just his imagination, Daniel felt a little more confident in asking her opinion. "So, what do you think about travelling back in time?"

"What a wonderful opportunity," she said. "I'd give my eyeteeth to do something like that. Just wish there was a way."

She eyed Daniel closely, as if trying to penetrate into his mind. He was sure she was searching for evidence of his planning to make another trip. But he kept silent, ducking his head so she couldn't peer into his eyes. He wasn't about to say anything about his plans to go again. Mr. Pederson was heading in their direction, so they began discussing special finds that had been discovered over the years.

The two older folks became so excited as they talked about archeological sites they'd worked on together that Daniel found himself totally hooked into going back to the time of the dinosaurs and staying longer than a few minutes. He might as well make his preparations worthwhile and make it a proper expedition to locate the *Edmontosaurus*. For sure, this would be his last excursion into the past.

Then he heard Dr. Roost say she would make the trip into town for more plaster of Paris. They hoped to bring in some of the smaller fossils by the end of the day.

"But I won't need to wrap any large fossils for quite some time, so there's no reason to make a special trip," Mr. Pederson said.

"I want to do this," Dr. Roost insisted.

"At least take my truck," Mr. Pederson persuaded her, holding out his keys. "Yours is your home. Mine is for hauling things."

Mildred grumbled something about male chauvinism, but took the keys and strutted off in quick fashion with her cane swinging.

Mr. Pederson went ahead to the quarry, while Daniel and the Nelwins finished at the barn. An hour later, the brothers left for the dig site. Daniel gathered bottles of water and his own tools and was ready to head out too, but Mom intercepted him. She gave him a container of snacks for their mid-morning break. Dr. Roost had still not shown up by then. Daniel walked anxiously to the end of the driveway and peered down the access road. He returned wistfully.

"You go ahead," Jed called to him, "I'll help her when she comes."

"Okay, thanks," Daniel agreed without a moment's hesitation. He was anxious to check on the progress of uncovering the *Stygimoloch*. Peculiar, though, that Dr. Roost wasn't back yet. From all the praises Mr. Pederson had given about her, being late was not one of her characteristics. Where could she be?

Once on the site, Daniel carefully removed the tarp from the *Stygimoloch* skull. He bent to examine it. Most of it was exposed, except for a back portion which was encased under heavy soil. They wouldn't be able to get to it until they'd dug down, and getting to that depth meant digging more layered steps – the main reason Pederson had brought the Nelwins to help. Daniel covered the skull again. He guessed they wouldn't be wrapping it for a few days yet.

Daniel moved over to his own section and picked up a small paintbrush. Softly, he brushed around several teeth on a raised area about thirty centimetres in diameter. A shallow trench surrounded it. As he worked, he uncovered a piece of the jaw close to several teeth. Excitedly, he called Mr. Pederson over.

"Good work, lad!" Pederson said, coming up behind him. "We might as well take this segment in. I have enough plaster for it."

Daniel picked up a small trowel and began digging the trench deeper and cutting away the dirt underneath and around the segment of fossils, forming a pedestal like a giant mushroom.

From above them, the Nelwins stopped and leaned on their shovels.

"Why are you doing that?" Craig called out.

"It strengthens and protects the teeth for when we transport them," Daniel answered, sitting back on his haunches, satisfied with his work. "Come and watch if you want."

As the boys hurried down, Pederson brought over some tissue paper, strips of burlap, and a plaster of Paris mixture. Carefully, he and Daniel laid the tissue over the fossilized teeth, then dipped the burlap into the plaster and spread the strips overtop, sealing it well. While they waited for it the field jacket to dry, they trooped over to see the progress of the Nelwins.

"Great work, lads!" Mr. Pederson encouraged them.

Daniel noticed the boys flushing with pride. They probably didn't often hear any praise.

Daniel passed out bottles of water, and they stood sipping and staring out over the valley around them. The pale blue-grey of the distant hills gave them a restful feeling underneath the hazy sun of the late morning. A hawk swooped and swerved down the valley, giving out a harsh *keeer* cry. As they breathed deeply, the distinctive smell of sage scented the air. No one spoke for a time, letting the peacefulness wash over them.

The Nelwins eventually returned to their digging, and Mr. Pederson continued uncovering more of the *Stygimoloch*. While the plaster of the field jacket set, Daniel worked on an area close by. The heat and the dry winds sped up the drying process and he was soon able to move back to the partially jacketed teeth.

He began trenching farther underneath the fossils until the stem of the pedestal-shape was narrow enough to snap off and roll over. Pederson and the Nelwins came over to help him flip it. Then, Daniel cleared the base until he was close to the underside of the teeth. Together, they wrapped the bottom until the entire fossil clump was covered with the plaster jacket.

"Now what will you do with it?" Craig asked.

Mr. Pederson stood and answered. "Haul it back to the farm, then to the Royal Saskatchewan Museum lab at Eastend. The researchers and technicians will assemble and study it there."

"You mean you don't get to do that?" asked Todd.

"We're part of the team that prefers to keep digging for the time being," Pederson answered. "Besides, we have an agreement with the RSM and we're in good hands with Tim Tokaryk. They're the experts over there."

"Have you ever been there?" Daniel asked.

Todd and Craig shook their heads.

"How about we take you sometime?" Pederson said, obviously pleased with the Nelwins' interest in paleontology.

"Sure," said Craig, the more outgoing of the two. Todd nodded his head in agreement.

Suddenly, they all turned at the sound of some scuffling overhead.

"Ahoy, there!" A shout came from Mildred Roost, who appeared over the crest of the hill above them. They watched her progress as she ambled down skilfully, barely using her cane as a support. She reached the bottom unscathed and began leisurely examining the day's progress in the bone bed. Her face was partially hidden by her Tilley hat, but they could see a look of deep concentration etched there.

"So do I get to see your new find today?" she asked smiling hopefully.

Pederson took her arm and guided her to the *Stygimoloch* skull. She lifted the tarp and bent down to study the fossil. Her eyes brightened with excitement, as she turned to Ole Pederson. "This is a find of great consequence!"

"I have great hopes there will be far more of the skeleton here," Pederson said, pleased by her praise.

Mildred nodded. "Indeed, this find will bring you great recognition, and about time too!" She grasped him by the arm and he beamed at her.

They wandered over the site then, chatting in their own world, as if the rest of them didn't exist. The Nelwins went back to digging, and Daniel watched the old couple for a few minutes, wondering if there was something more than the shared interest in paleontology drawing them together.

Then he thought again about his trip to prehistoric time. Dr. Roost was definitely going to be an added distraction to everyone. He might try to go even sooner than he'd planned. He just had to make sure she didn't notice any suspicious movements. Her hawk-like eyes didn't seem to miss much! He'd be extremely careful around her while he gathered his gear.

Vials, specimen kits, labels! Daniel mentally added those to his list too. Maybe a first aid kit would be a good thing, especially as he seemed prone to being injured. And what about some kind of strong rope? He'd definitely take his binoculars and maybe a magnifying glass.

Although he'd decided to stay in the past more than a few minutes, he still didn't intend on being there long. He wasn't sure of the time changes from present to past, or what kind of terrain he'd end up in, and he might need to rest. A small nylon tent would be of little protection set up on the ground, so that was out. Maybe he should take a sheet of plastic that he could wrap around himself while he was up in a tree, in case it rained? He shuddered at the thought of spending hours in cramped conditions. He had no intention of doing that and quickly shrugged off the idea.

Jed appeared a few moments later, panting with the weight of the sack of plaster of Paris on his back. He slid the bag to the ground and groaned with relief. Then he joined Daniel, waving to the Nelwins on the hill above them.

"Hello, Jedlock!" Daniel gave him a high-five. "How's it going?"

"Good!" he said, rolling his shoulder blades together to ease the tension. "Hauling that plaster for Dr. Roost is not my idea of fun. But as far as the tours go, it's been a light morning. I'm sure it'll pick up this afternoon. We've had a few more calls."

Then Daniel explained what he'd done so far that day, pointing to the fossils in the field jacket drying in the sun.

"Do you think I could come back and work on my area sometime?" Jed asked, looking wistfully over at the tiny scratching marks of a bird-like creature he'd uncovered several days earlier. Prints of any kind were rare, and ones of birds almost non-existent, so these were extremely important.

"Sure," Daniel said. "Let's see the schedule when we get back, and maybe you can come later and I'll take over the tours."

"Right on!" Jed said, breaking into a huge grin.

As they observed the action below, they saw Dr. Roost take a digital camera from her backpack. She took a couple of shots of the tiny fossils, then wandered over and took some of the exposed ribs.

A digital camera! That's what I need, Daniel thought, wondering if he could borrow hers for his adventure into the past. He'd have instant results of everything he snapped, and wouldn't have to take extra rolls of film with him. Mentally, he reviewed his list. Could he fit everything into his backpack? He'd have to make it so.

The Nelwins worked at a slower pace now that the sun was higher in the sky. Mildred Roost wandered off, scouring the hillsides. Daniel and Pederson began gathering the tiny fossils from the microsite. They scooped shovelfuls carefully into gunny sacks, ready to take to the lab with the jacketed teeth fossils.

The rest of the morning passed quickly. Dr. Roost eventually returned and they all headed back to the farmyard for lunch. There was time to have a nice long break before more tourists arrived.

Daniel, Lucy, and Jed looked over the schedule after finishing their meals. They saw that they could handle all the tours and still give Jed some time at the site. Jed decided to leave right away, so he could extend his time. Mr. Pederson, Mildred Roost, and the Nelwins headed off with him.

As they passed by Daniel's dad, he quietly stopped Craig and Todd.

"Thanks for the great job you've done today, boys," he said.

"You're welcome," they replied in unison, their voices sounding surprised. They seemed to stand a little straighter.

"I don't mind doing farm work," Todd said.

"Good," Dad answered, with a kindly dismissive gesture. "Have fun at the dig."

"We will," answered Craig, before he and Todd rushed to catch up with the others.

While everyone was distracted, Daniel slipped away to plan for his trip. The worst problem would be keeping safe. Taking any kind of weapon would be useless against the megabeasts he'd encounter. Big knives, bows and arrows, and guns of any sort – regular, machine, elephant, or tranquillizers – wouldn't be enough, even if he had access to any and knew how to use them. Dinosaurs' hides were just too thick, and dinosaurs were too large to be brought down with a couple of shots. There weren't even any steep cliffs to run them over like the First Nations people had done to buffalo in the past. Besides they were far bigger creatures. He shivered at the thought of being attacked. What would he do? He had to think of something or he'd be dino food in a flash.

CHAPTER SIX

I n his room, Daniel finalized his list and quietly began gathering the gear for the trip. In the bathroom, he loaded up with the bug spray, sunscreen, and first aid stuff. He slid open his closet door and laid them out on the bottom shelf. Mom wouldn't be doing laundry for a while, so no one should see his stash.

From his computer desk, he retrieved pencils, pens, sketching paper, and a notebook. As he collected all the items on the list, he ticked them off. When he'd done what he could in his room, Daniel headed to the kitchen. He rummaged around for some waterproof matches and grabbed a stash of granola bars. They would be light and easy to pack. He'd need something more substantial, but he could easily find something when he was ready to leave. Mom was used to him loading up and going out to the excavation site or his hideout. And really, this wouldn't be any different, except he'd be going to visit the dinosaurs live!

In the porch, he grabbed a couple of plastic garbage bags. The tools he wanted to take were at his hideout, and that was where he'd leave from. He thought again about using Dr. Roost's digital camera instead of his own regular film one. A video camera would be even better, but no one he knew had one. Dr. Roost's would do nicely. He just had to think of a way of asking for it without raising any suspicions.

Daniel returned to his closet and lined everything up according to survival, research, and personal items. He felt his pulse race as he thought of his expedition. Maybe he should go tonight? No, being in prehistoric time in the dark was probably not the smartest thing to do. He'd noticed that no one was booked for a tour until eleven tomorrow. Maybe he could go after morning chores? He could go even earlier, if he could get the Nelwins to cover his barn chores for him.

Excitedly, Daniel plotted his trip. He was positive he'd end up in the same prehistoric period, because he had the pine cone from that time. And he felt reasonably sure that he'd end up in the general vicinity of where he'd been three times before. As soon as he arrived, though, he'd have to be prepared to find cover quickly. He would be in constant danger, but he'd just have to be smarter than the dinosaurs!

Speaking of which, he'd need to get some strong rope and plastic tape for marking his trail. There was some of it around from the dig site, because they used it to indicate potential find sites and for cordoning off areas, but he wasn't sure there was enough left. Instead, he'd take his mom's narrower green plant tape that she used to tie up her sweetpeas and other trailing vegetation. She wouldn't be looking for it yet. He'd get those items later.

With nothing left to do immediately for the trip, Daniel joined the others outside where they waited for the first afternoon tour to assemble. Soon they were back in the rhythm of taking tourists on tours and trails. Daniel took their guests on the horse trails, and the afternoon flew swiftly by.

In the early evening, Daniel approached the Nelwins while they were outside feeding the stock in the pasture. Todd looked up when he approached. Craig was on the other side of the cattle, pouring chop into another trough.

"How's it going?" Daniel asked, trying to be casual.

"Okay, I guess," Todd looked at him guardedly.

"Look, I was, uh, wondering, if maybe, uh, I could ask you to do me a small favour?" Daniel stumbled through his request. He'd have to do better than that if he didn't want them guessing the importance of what he was up to.

"I don't know," said Todd. "What is it?"

"Well, I sort of have something really important I need to do early tomorrow morning," Daniel leaned casually against a fence post. "I was just wondering if you'd consider taking care of all of my chores – you know, do the milking, and separating, and all?"

Todd grimaced. "I suppose. We still owe you." He called over to Craig, "Daniel wants us to do his chores tomorrow."

"Shhhh!" Daniel said, noticing that Mildred Roost had come out of nowhere and was crossing the yard.

"Ahh! A secret. What are you *really* up to?" Todd said, suspiciously, as Craig arrived.

"Nothing much. I just want an early start is all." He shrugged his shoulders and pretended what he wanted wasn't any big deal. All he needed was for his cover to be blown!

"Think you're about to find something special after today's digging?" asked Craig, keenly interested.

"Yeah," Daniel said reluctantly. "It does have to do with a little paleontology research." That was the truth. So what, if they thought it had to do with the quarry? He was going to relatively the same place, only a few million years earlier.

"Sure, I guess," Craig said. Todd nodded.

"Only what if someone asks where you are?" Todd eyed Daniel apprehensively. "Do we tell them?"

Daniel tried to act nonchalant. "Sure. If I'm not there, then I'll be at my hideout." He figured that if anyone went to look for him and couldn't find him at one place, it would take them a while to look in the other. He could always say he had gone off prospecting, or was some-where in between the two places.

As Daniel left to feed the horses, he could feel Craig's curious eyes on him. His heart pounded in his chest. So far, so good, the chores were covered. Now he just had to devise the rest of the plan. He'd noticed there were quite a few sandwiches left over from lunch today, so he could probably snag a few without anyone noticing. He had a back-up plan in mind too. Whistling, he finished his chores.

He still was whistling as he headed back to the house, where he encountered Pederson.

"You seem mighty pleased about something, lad," Pederson stared at him in sudden surprise. "Anything you'd like to share?

"Just plenty of exciting things going on, I guess." Daniel skirted a direct answer.

Pederson squinted at Daniel disbelievingly, but said nothing for a few moments.

"So, what's the next step with the *Stygimoloch*?" asked Daniel, trying to divert attention from himself.

"We definitely need more of the overburden removed to get to the entire skeleton."

"Let me help," Daniel suggested.

"No, you're not ready."

"But..."

Suddenly, Daniel became quiet. He didn't want to promise to go too early in the morning, as he didn't know when he'd return from the past. He shrugged.

"Okay, I'll give myself another day."

Pederson looked at him in surprise for a few moments, but then turned to acknowledge Dr. Roost, who had joined them again. Daniel stayed with them politely for a few minutes, but he was anxious to double-check that he had everything, and to pack. While the adults talked, he thought about his plans. With all the extra people around the farm these days and the Nelwins covering for him, his absence would probably go unnoticed. Wouldn't it be fantastic if he could find a *Stygimoloch* and maybe even get a photograph?

Mr Pederson gave him a gentle poke in the ribs. "Right, Daniel?"

Daniel brought his focus back to Mildred Roost and Mr. Pederson. He didn't have a clue what they were discussing.

"Uh, sorry, sir. What were you saying?" he asked, realizing they were both staring at him.

"Nothing important, lad. You looked like you were millions of miles from here. What are you thinking about so intensely?"

Daniel's thought whirled. What could he say?

"The *Stygimoloch*," he blurted out. "I was just imagining what they might be like in real life." He stumbled over his explanation. "For no particular reason." Every time he opened his mouth, he was making it worse.

Mildred Roost stared at Daniel curiously, her interest radar suddenly perking up. He shifted uncomfortably. She shot Daniel another questioning look. Pederson's eyes narrowed slightly, but he didn't say anything.

Daniel added quickly, "I just think they're interesting is all."

"I agree," said Dr. Roost.

She seemed about to say something else, but Pederson interrupted. "Well, I don't know about the rest of you, but I'm hungry. Shall we go, Mildred?"

Dr. Roost nodded. They were going into Eastend for supper at Jack's Café. Daniel almost wished he were going with them. There was something exciting about being surrounded by a panoramic landscape, depicting the history of the area from the early years of civilization to modern-day technology, while eating great food – their pizzas and garlic bread were scrumptious.

"We'll say good night then, Daniel, because it will probably be late when we return and we don't want to keep you from anything important," Pederson said. He had a strange gleam in his eyes as he guided Mildred towards his vehicle.

"Good night for now, Daniel," Mildred echoed Pederson's suspicious mood with a raise of her eyebrow.

That was a close one, Daniel thought. Those two early risers were the ones he'd have to avoid the most in the morning. Hopefully, he'd be long gone in the morning before they could notice and spoil his plans!

Then Daniel remembered he needed to ask about borrowing Dr. Roost's digital camera. He hurried after them, although he wasn't sure if she'd agree to such a big favour.

Daniel reached Dr. Roost just as she opened the truck door.

"Dr. Roost?" Daniel puffed.

"Yes, Daniel," she said, surprised by his approach.

"Uh, I was just wondering if I could ask you something? Sort of a favour," Daniel said.

Dr. Roost shoved her Tilley onto her forehead, leaned on her cane, and gave Daniel her full attention. Mr. Pederson waited patiently by his side of the truck, watching them.

"What is it?" Dr. Roost asked.

"Well, I noticed, uh, that you have a digital camera, and I was wondering, well," Daniel hesitated, "well, if you might consider lending it to me for a short time."

Mildred Roost eyed him sternly.

"When and why?" she demanded.

"Early tomorrow morning," Daniel shot out. "I wanted to get an early start and I thought maybe it would be good to get some photographs before the tourists arrived," Daniel stretched the truth again. "I figured if I took digital ones, then I could store them on my computer." That part was definitely true.

She shifted her cane, calculating his reasons. She pursed her lips, stared hard at him, and nodded. "Okay, but I expect it back in the condition I give it to you."

"Yes, ma'am," Daniel said, surprised that she'd agreed so easily.

She swung her canvas backpack off her shoulder, and dug out the camera. "Do you know how to use it?"

"I think so." Daniel took it from her and looked at it. She pointed out a few things to him. He experimented by taking a shot of Mr. Pederson, leaning against the hood of his truck with his arms crossed over his chest. They examined the results on the screen on the side.

"Go on with you, then, Daniel," she said, tapping him gently on his arm with her cane.

"Yes, ma'am," he said again, as he tried to avoid her eyes while hurrying off.

Wow! He actually had a digital camera. He could take great photos and even put them on the Internet. Then everyone would have to believe him! He watched Mr. Pederson and Dr. Roost drive out of the yard, giving them a final wave before he turned back to the house. He hurried to tuck the camera into his closet with the rest of his gear. Then he joined everyone outside for a barbecue to celebrate the successful first weekend of their venture.

Later that evening, the Nelwins and Lindstroms gathered their belongings and began heading for home as the sun's rays cascaded over the farm buildings in warm orange tones. A slight breeze rustled the poplar leaves, and a pleasant quiet settled over the farm. In the distance, they heard the muted voices of the campers from halfway down the valley, preparing for after-dark campfires and marshmallow roasts.

In his bedroom, Daniel spread everything out on his bed. He took inventory as he began stuffing the items into his backpack, making sure everything was compactly pushed down so he could fit it all in.

A sudden knock on his bedroom door sent Daniel scrambling. He whipped the quilt off with everything inside it and threw it into his closet, along with the backpack, and slid the door shut. Then he messed up his sheets as if he'd been lying down.

"Daniel?" Mom said, knocking again. "What are you doing in there?"

"Just getting ready for bed," he called. "Just a minute."

Daniel opened the door to let her in, holding his pyjamas in his hand as if he was just getting changed. "Hi, Mom," he said nonchalantly.

Mom had that concerned look on her face again.

"Are you feeling all right?" She felt his forehead. "Your face is flushed. I hope you're not coming down with something."

"Nah, I'm fine," he said, standing in the doorway and unfolding his pyjamas. Anything to keep her from noticing his missing quilt.

"Maybe you should take it a little easier tomorrow." Mom suggested.

Daniel couldn't believe his good fortune. Here was an opening he couldn't give up.

"How about if I hang out at my hideout for a while in the morning? I wouldn't mind putting it right," he suggested, hoping Mom would agree. If she did, then anyone who happened to see him go wouldn't question the load he was carrying.

Mom thought about it for a few minutes. "I suppose that would be okay. As long as you don't do anything strenuous. You need to give your body time to mend."

"I'll be fine, Mom," Daniel said. "Just a little walking, some puttering, maybe some picture taking." What he planned to do was all true, just not exactly in the current time.

Mom gave Daniel a quick hug and a kiss goodnight on his forehead, then left the room. Daniel breathed a sigh of relief as his heart pounded in his chest. That had been too close for comfort.

Then a sudden stab of guilt hit him as he thought about how he was taking advantage of his mom's trust. He felt bad about not telling her the truth, but she'd never believe him. He shook the moment off, and rushed over to his closet. He was just about to open it, when Mom appeared at his door again.

"How about turning off your light right away and getting some sleep?"

"Okay," Daniel smiled, and shrugged his shoulders. "Not a problem."

Mom left again. Whew! He'd have to be more careful. This time he listened through his door to make sure his mom had gone back downstairs. Then he quickly finished repacking. He hid the backpack far back in the closet, draping an old sweater over it to make it look like it had fallen down accidentally. He rearranged the hangers full of clothes to hide the whole lump.

He set his alarm and changed into his pyjamas. But Daniel knew he couldn't sleep yet. His thoughts were clanging in his head, and his body practically vibrated with his excitement. Everything was in place. He couldn't wait to go.

Turning out his lights, he pulled a chair over to his open window. He opened the blinds and raised the window higher to let in more of the calm night air. He gazed out over the farmyard at the pasture beyond. Crickets chirped by the buildings, and farther away he could hear frogs *ribbiting* near the dugout.

Calming his mind somewhat, he finally headed for bed. He lay there going over his plans, determined to make the most of his experience. Without realizing it, he sank into sleep.

CHAPTER SEVEN

Daniel's muffled alarm rang at 4:30 in the morning. He shut it off and pulled it out from underneath his pillow. The sky was already becoming filled with early morning light. Quietly, he dressed and gathered his belongings. As he snuck down the stairs, he avoided the one creaky step, and made it to the kitchen without turning on any lights. Opening the fridge a crack, he pulled out some sandwiches and bottles of water. Quickly, he zipped them inside the front flap of his backpack.

Once outside, he stared up at the bedroom windows, but couldn't see anyone about. Dactyl appeared from under the step. He yawned and stretched, then padded over to Daniel.

Already, Daniel had a problem. He'd forgotten about his dog. Dactyl wouldn't stay behind, and locking his pet into the barn wouldn't help – the dog would bark and wake everyone up. The only thing he could do was let him come, then hope to distract him with food temporarily when he made the leap into the past.

Keeping in the shadows close to the buildings, Daniel made it across the farmyard to his mom's garden shed. He had to make one fast stop. As gently as he could, he opened the squeaky door. He held his breath and looked again at the house, then slipped inside the gloomy darkness.

Luckily, he knew approximately where the roll of plastic banding tape should be and was able to walk over to it. He couldn't see much of anything, but used his hands to rummage through a couple of boxes. At last, he felt the roll. He grabbed it and slid it into a side pouch of his backpack.

Warily, he slid back outside and pushed the workshop door closed as quietly as he could. Streaks of light radiated on the horizon, as he walked past the barn. Not long afterwards, Dactyl disappeared chasing some gophers. As quick as he could, Daniel covered the hills and descended to his hideout.

He was just about to crawl inside, when he heard a voice that made him drop his backpack.

"I knew you were up to something." Mildred Roost came forward from the shadows on the side of the hideout.

Daniel couldn't speak. His heart felt like a bowling ball stuck in his throat.

"So, young man, please tell me that you're not doing what I think you're doing." Dr. Roost tilted her head and waited for Daniel to respond.

He didn't want to tell a lie and he couldn't speak the truth.

"There is no way you are going anywhere other than home, young man!" Dr. Roost insisted, guessing his intent.

Daniel stood defiantly, facing her.

"I have to go," he said adamantly. "There's only this one chance to prove a few things that are really important to Mr. Pederson and I."

"They may be important to Ole, but he would never want you to risk your life!" Mildred Roost countered.

"But it's my decision. Besides, I don't plan on getting in any trouble!" Daniel declared.

"I'd suggest you let me go instead," suggested Dr. Roost. "It's too dangerous for you, Daniel."

"Dangerous for you too," he blurted out.

"I'm an old lady," she said. "I've lived my life, and haven't much to lose now. You still have your whole life ahead of you."

"Aren't you afraid of dying?" Daniel asked.

Mildred Roost explained. "I don't want to die, but I know it's coming and I'm as prepared for it as I can be."

"No offence, but you'd never be able to get away from the dinosaurs in time," Daniel said honestly, thinking about her age and her use of a cane.

"I'm sure game to try," she persisted. "Besides, it would be the most fantastic thing I could do in my whole life. What a glorious way to end it, if it came to that."

Daniel stared at her open-mouthed.

"If you think it's safe enough for you, young man, it'll be fine for me."

"But you might have to climb a tree," Daniel pointed out as he tried to picture Mildred Roost climbing one of the huge trees. He'd have laughed if the situation wasn't so serious. "There isn't anywhere else to get away from them."

"I'm sure I have a few tricks up my sleeve," she said confidently, patting her backpack.

There was no way Daniel was letting her go without him after all his planning.

"I'm not without experience in dangerous situations, you know," she declared. "Just tell me how to get there, and I'll be off."

Daniel shook his head. "But I know the way to the *Edmontosaurus*."

"I'm sure I can find her – you just need to give me directions," said Dr. Roost.

"I *have* to go," Daniel pleaded.

"Daniel, you have to listen to reason," implored Dr. Roost. "You'd be sorely missed if you didn't return. And I'd never forgive myself."

Daniel thought about his family for a moment, but convinced himself that he would be okay.

He stood his ground. "I'm definitely going!"

Mildred Roost shuffled her weight and stared at him intently. "How about a compromise then, Daniel?" she suggested.

Daniel eyed her with curiosity.

"How about you and I both go?"

Now Daniel felt like the bowling ball had settled into his stomach. She could ruin everything. She would be nothing but trouble, slowing him down.

"I won't even be gone long," Daniel explained. "I'll just pop into the past and go straight to the *Edmontosaurus* to see if she's the same one we uncovered," he said. "And I'm hoping I can take a photo of the *Stygimoloch*. Otherwise, I'll be right back. You'd hardly have time to see anything."

Dr. Roost cleared her throat. "I'm not sure you have much choice in the matter," she said with rigid determination. "If you're going, young man, so am I."

Daniel felt panic pulsing along his veins. She could be about as delicate as a rhinoceros in a henhouse, and just about as noisy too. Did he dare tell her what he thought?

She seemed to read his mind. "I'll go along quietly, let you take the lead. At least if I'm there, maybe I can keep you safe."

Daniel shook his head, stifling a bout of nervous laughter. It would be everything he could do to keep *her* out of harm's way. What if she got hurt or was killed?

"It's just too dangerous for you to come!" Daniel blurted out.

Ignoring his protests, Dr. Roost adjusted her bulging backpack and stood with her arms crossed in front of her.

Daniel studied her. Today she wore baggy trousers with a long, camel-coloured shirt and sturdy walking boots. Under her Tilley hat, her long grey hair was caught up in a braid that she'd wound around her head. She was definitely attired for the trip. But she couldn't possibly help him and would probably get in his way!

As if sensing his thoughts, Mildred Roost added, "I can keep pace with you well enough. I can assist you too. One of us will keep our eyes peeled in all directions, while the other takes photographs or gathers information. We can improvise as we go."

Daniel looked at her in surprise.

"Oh yes, I've been doing a lot of thinking about this," she said excitedly. "This is the chance of a lifetime, and I'm going to make the most of it! You know the terrain, right?"

Daniel nodded. "Yes, but it's quite a hike through trees and sloughy land."

"Let's do it, then," she replied.

Daniel knew she wasn't going to budge. He'd either have to take her along or forget it, at least for awhile. Or maybe for good – if Mildred Roost told Mr. Pederson or his parents.

"We still need to be inside my hideout, though, to leave." He looked at her questioningly.

Mildred Roost swung her backpack off and slid it into the hideout doorway, followed by her cane. Then she got down on her hands and knees and crawled inside. Daniel shoved his backpack in next, and followed behind. Mildred Roost knelt as she surveyed the interior of his hideout.

"Wow, this is superb, Daniel. When we return, you'll have to tell me about the contents." She gave a husky laugh, as she looked around at his collections of stones and fossils, and his overnight gear. Then she stood up in the centre and slipped her backpack on and waited for Daniel's instructions.

"So how does this work?" Dr. Roost asked.

He pointed to the wall. "I have a pine cone from the past hidden there. You'll have to hang on to me, because as soon as I touch it, we'll be hurled into the Cretaceous time."

"Amazing," said Dr. Roost. "Well, let's go!"

Daniel felt suddenly nervous. It was one thing to go alone, but to purposely take someone else that he was responsible for wasn't part of his plan for adventure. With Dr. Roost watching his every move, his self-assurance seemed to slip. He had to concentrate on the task instead and bolster his own confidence. Besides being a momentous occasion, he knew how dangerous the trip was. Dr. Roost seemed to sense the seriousness. She stood still and silent, allowing Daniel to prepare himself mentally for their journey.

Daniel stared at Mildred Roost intently. He should have little trouble convincing her of danger or when to return, unlike the problem he'd had with the Nelwins.

They'd been so scared and disbelieving that they'd almost destroyed the chance to make it back. He'd just stay close to Dr. Roost and make sure they came back together. Her coming along changed his plans, though – she'd probably slow him down.

"We have to stick really close together, and if we're in any danger, we have to drop the cone and we'll be back here instantly." Just saying that out loud somehow made him feel safer.

"I understand totally, Daniel," Dr. Roost confirmed quietly.

Daniel's palms were sweaty and his heart thumped loudly as he moved about gathering the tools he needed and stowing them in his backpack. He went over to his stump and sat down. He stared at the patched wall where the pine cone was hidden, reassuring himself that he was only going for a short time. Just long enough to track down the *Edmontosaurus,* take a few pictures of any *Stygimoloch* they might see, and gather a few samples along the way.

Daniel looked at her. "Be ready to dash off in any direction as soon as we arrive," he directed her.

She nodded.

Reaching for the small garden trowel, Daniel clutched it firmly and stood up. Now was the time for action. He began scraping the patched dirt off the wall. *Clink!* He hit the stone covering the pine cone. He gulped. Gently, he pried out the stone and set down the trowel, pushing both away with his foot, while keeping his eyes on the hole.

Swiftly, Daniel checked his pockets and adjusted his backpack. He was all set. If his theory was right, they should end up about where he'd been before. Hopefully, they wouldn't land in the water, or they'd be at a disadvantage right from the start. He glanced over at Dr. Roost.

She showed him a thumbs-up signal. Her eyes danced with anticipation as she moved to stand beside him.

"Stick right with me and move fast if you need to," he warned again. "Now hold onto my hand."

She reached out and took his left hand, giving it a squeeze. She held her cane in her other hand and stood looking straight ahead and ready for action.

Taking a deep breath, Daniel reached for the pine cone. Out of the corner of his eye, he saw Dactyl appear in the doorway. There was no time to lose!

In one sudden, jerking movement, Daniel grabbed for the cone. At the same time, Dr. Roost tightened her grip on his hand. A sizzling crack sounded in his ears. A split second later everything went black.

Daniel and Mildred Roost were in prehistoric time!

Daniel gasped in the hot, humid air, twisting his head this way and that, trying to take everything in at once. He heard Mildred Roost's sharp intake of breath as she suddenly dropped his hand. Not seeing any immediate danger, Daniel tucked the pine cone into his jeans pocket, and watched in delight as Dr. Roost took in her surroundings, her mouth open in astonishment. Dawn was just breaking and streaks of yellow and pink lit up the sky.

They'd landed almost on target on the shore of a huge inland sea. Daniel was sure it was the same one, because it stretched far into the horizon and familiar-looking streams spilled into the muddy shore. Densely crowded small trees, low bushes, and ferns grew along the water's edge.

Luckily, they hadn't landed right in the water. Unfortunately, though, their feet were stuck in gooey mud. Dr. Roost stood rooted in the soft mud as if held there by hardened cement. When Daniel tried to lift a sneaker, he had to pull hard against the sucking sludge. His movements roused Dr. Roost, who wrestled herself free with her cane, now firmly gripped in her right hand.

Gradually, they moved farther onto the beach, steadying each other. They scraped the muck off their shoes, but not before some had oozed inside and got on their socks and pant legs. Mildred Roost didn't even seem to notice the discomfort as she observed their environment.

"Bloody amazing!" Her quiet words were full of wonder.

Sudden, piercing sounds penetrated the air from the

depths of the dark forest in front of them. The first light of dawn sent shadows over the beachfront from a single lofty pine close by.

"Daniel, look!" Dr. Roost pointed to a *Basilemys*, one of the largest turtles known from the period. "It must be a metre and a half long and a metre across."

As they watched, the creature poked its neck farther out of its thick shell, raised its head, and squinted at them with tiny eyes. Its fat, tubular legs lay flat to the ground with flapper-like feet on the ends that presumably pushed the mud as it plodded along.

"Graviportal legs, just like some turtles today," observed Dr. Roost. Then she explained. "They can't move their wrists and ankles, because the heavy shell restricts their limbs from ever becoming vertical."

"That's why they move so slowly, I guess," Daniel said. "That shell is as thick as my fist!" He studied its hard covering, marvelling at the distinctive patterns etched into it, as it turned and lumbered along the shore away from them.

Towards the water's edge on a low branch of a gingko tree, a large gull-like bird groomed its multicoloured feathers with its long, tooth-filled beak. Suddenly, it flew off and snapped up a giant green beetle scuttling along the mud.

Mildred Roost grasped her hands together in excitement. "I can hardly believe this is real," she said softly, so as not to attract attention to them.

Around a distant point of the shoreline, some kind of creatures unfamiliar to Daniel roamed. He pointed them out to Dr. Roost, as they ripped at aquatic plants. In between their long necks and whip-like tails, their bodies were protected by bony plates. They had four stump-like legs, long skulls with large ear openings, and wide snouts for gobbling plants.

"If I didn't know better, I'd think we were seeing *Quaesitosaurus*," Mildred Roost spoke quietly beside him. "But they lived much earlier and only in Mongolia, so these must be some kind of related species."

Daniel eyed the large creatures warily, and then he noticed a flock of large shorebirds on the beach.

"*Cimolopteryx*, I think," Daniel pointed.

"Remarkable!" said Dr. Roost. "Remains have only been found as close as Wyoming up until now."

They watched the colourful prehistoric birds use their long, slender bills to probe in the mud for food. Occasionally one waded into the water and then dove after its prey, running rapidly on long, strong legs. They took no notice of the humans.

As Daniel surveyed the environment, he reflected on the strangeness of being in a place where almost all the animals were unfamiliar. There were no cows, horses, cats, or dogs. All of those would come many millions of years later. How amazing to be standing there watching creatures that were extinct in his own time! Their world had to disappear for his world to evolve into what it was today.

He looked in the other direction, further down the seaside, where two creatures about the size of an ostrich were drinking in the shallows. They had five-fingered hands on small arms, and four-toed feet at the back. Daniel took note of the horny beaks and large eyes protruding from their smallish heads. They must have come to the freshwater sea to quench their thirst, as they usually lived in the forest.

"My goodness, I can't believe my eyes – *Thescelosaurus*," Mildred spoke at last.

Daniel nodded. He'd seen examples of *Thescelosaurus* on his last trip and had recognized them then.

"The only traces of a dinosaur heart that's ever been found came from one of them. They discovered it in a fossilized chest cavity down in South Dakota. It was four-chambered, so they think they were warm-blooded creatures, although some scientists more recently have challenged this theory."

"Wow!" said Daniel, looking at them with renewed interest. "I didn't know that."

"I'm not too surprised to see that they lived around here, I just wonder why we haven't come across any fossils of them so far." She poked Daniel. "Get out the camera."

As quietly as he could, Daniel fished the camera out of his backpack and handed it to Dr. Roost. He'd let her do the picture taking, while he kept watch. So far, they were only seeing relatively harmless herbivores and bird-like creatures. Not that Daniel was complaining. And although they'd only been here less than a couple of minutes, he knew he had to find a safe vantage point for them soon.

Daniel kept watch for *Borealosuchus* – huge crocodiles – behind them, but he knew from experience that it was hard to distinguish them from the fallen logs on the beach and those draping into the water. If something moved suddenly, they'd have to make a run for it. They'd have to keep their eyes skyward too. He peered into the redwood forest several hundred yards away.

Normally, he would have made his way to one of the trees that he could climb to safety, but now that he had Mildred Roost to consider, he'd aim instead for a huge clump of cycads. Not the best choice, but at least some ground cover would protect them from sight. They had some dangerous patches to cross before they would get to the nesting *Edmontosaurus*. Would they make it there unscathed?

For the moment, danger seemed far away and he felt the thrill of being back in this marvellous world. And this time he had someone with him who understood what they were seeing and who might even be of help to him.

CHAPTER EIGHT

Back down the beach, Daniel saw the *Thescelosaurus* turning away from the sea and heading back into the trees. A flock of pterosaurs scooped fish out of the shallow water some distance away. To their left, creatures that looked like a cross between a loon and a huge duck crowded onto the shore on their bellies like penguins. They only seemed to be able to move by digging into the sand with their legs and pushing like a sea turtle. They obviously couldn't fly.

Daniel became mesmerized as he watched some of them plough rapidly through the water with sharp leg strokes. They dove underwater, using long jaws filled with many tiny teeth to grab at schools of fish. Their feathered bodies were sleek with long legs and webbed feet. While they scanned the depths, they floated.

"They're *Hesperornis*-like," Dr. Roost said in his ear. "Look at their small wings. At most, they might use them to make turns while swimming under water, but see how they seem to rely on slowing down and using sideward strokes of their legs."

Daniel nodded. "And look at how their legs stick out – perpendicular to their bodies!"

"Definitely peculiar-looking!" Mildred Roost concurred.

Daniel chuckled quietly. "But then almost everything's really strange here!"

Dr. Roost gave a snort of agreement and snapped several more photographs. Daniel pulled his attention away and looked around for some way of marking their location on the beach. He wanted to be sure they could come back to their landing spot when they were ready to go back to their own time, so they could return to his hideout.

Touching Dr. Roost's arm, he whispered, "Your turn to keep watch. It's time to start marking our trail."

Quickly, he gathered some soggy limbs on the beach, standing them upright, and pounding several into the soft ground near a pine tree, teepee fashion. He tied them into a bundle with a chunk of twine he'd brought. All the while he worked, Dr. Roost seemed mesmerized by the environment.

"This is kind of like being in Florida, in the swampy areas," she said quietly.

"Have you been there?" Daniel asked.

"Yes, it's a fascinating place."

"I'd like to go there some day."

"I'm sure you shall," she said not taking her eyes off their surroundings. "Though this does have quite a few differences. Everything here is magnified in size and almost surreal compared to there."

"I don't suppose there's any place on earth that's like this," agreed Daniel, ducking a palm-sized bumblebee-like insect that flew at his head. "It's like everything is out of proportion here. Like we're little kids in a giant world."

Carefully, Daniel wound some of his mom's plant tape around his structure. Then he stood back and surveyed the result.

Dr. Roost tapped the structure with her cane. "Seems sturdy enough."

Daniel looked at her with one raised eyebrow in surprise. She hadn't offered any help or advice and he wasn't expecting her to pass judgement on his work. He ignored the comment and retrieved his compass, a pencil, and a scribbler. Drawing a rough map, he noted the direction they would be heading.

Mildred Roost came over to stand beside him as he tucked his notebook away. "This is better than I could ever have dreamed," she said.

"There's plenty more to see," Daniel answered as he slid the compass into his jeans pocket.

Carefully, he moved forward, motioning to Dr. Roost. She slung her camera strap around her neck and followed, making as little disturbance as possible, just as he did. The many small creatures in the underbrush could be dangerous too. He knew there had to be several hundred species in the prehistoric past, although maybe not as many as there were in the present world. For sure, dinosaurs shared their world with a multitude of others in various shapes and sizes: amphibians, tiny mammals, bony fishes and shellfishes, marine, land, and flying reptiles, insects, and birds.

And except for those he'd previously encountered, Daniel had no idea how any of them would react to human beings. Would they ignore them, or attack? He kept watch in all directions. If they were stung or bitten, who knew if they'd survive? If any of these creatures had poisonous venom, there probably wasn't an antidote, even in his own world. He swallowed and pushed forward through the tangled undergrowth. Their biggest challenge lay just ahead.

Without speaking, Daniel and Mildred Roost stumbled forward over rough terrain, through tall woody plants and knots of vegetation. When they made it to the outer edge of the treeline, they stopped to rest under a clump of giant cycad ferns. The air was humid and the day already hot although the sun had not yet fully risen. They mopped the sweat off their brows and retrieved their water bottles, taking deep drinks to refresh themselves.

"The variety of vegetation is incredible," said Dr. Roost, peering out of the fronds at magnolia trees, huge redwoods, flowering bushes, and rampant vines that twined throughout their surroundings. The foliage was lush and green beyond belief.

"Look at the height of those horsetails." She referred to a stand of thirty-metre trees that resembled giant asparagus plants.

"Do you know these are one of the plants that survived from prehistoric time? They're dwarf-like now, though," Mildred Roost said.

Daniel nodded. From everything he had read, many of the major groupings of plants that evolved during the Later Cretaceous period were closely related to today's flora. He mentioned this fact to Dr. Roost.

"Yes. And there's the proof," she agreed. "You'd almost think we were in some exotic place like southern China, instead of staring at the landscape of sixty-five million years before our time. That is, until you look at the creatures," she chuckled softly, pointing back the way they'd come.

The seashore was still active with strange reptiles sipping at the water's edge and bird-like creatures prodding for food in the sand with long, thin, pointy beaks. Dr. Roost grabbed her camera again and shot the world around them from every angle she could manage. Together they watched huge moths and bees with bulging eyes dipping into flourishing blossoms. One flew up to them, almost touching Daniel's face, but they were neither food nor danger, and it soon flew off.

Iridescent gold and green dragonflies hovered nearby, some of them with wings spanning as wide as Daniel could spread his one arm to the side of his body. The forest echoed with sharp screeches, low drones and rustlings, snapping trees, and an eerie, cawing clamour.

"Maybe we should move on," Daniel suggested after a few moments. They could take more time once they'd accomplished their mission and had found a safe haven. "I'd like to get to the *Edmontosaurus* before our luck runs out."

"Agreed," said Mildred.

As Daniel pressed his way through the lush, dark undergrowth, he carefully pushed back branches and huge leaves, taking stock of the situation before he stepped forward. Mildred followed his lead and kept quiet, moving only when he signalled it was safe to do so. Occasionally, she flicked at a crawling or flying insect that threatened to land on one of them. Her cane came in handy for pushing aside vegetation too.

Suddenly, Daniel rounded a bush and came to an abrupt stop. They'd almost broad-sided an *Ankylosaurus*. It stood tank-like. Its heavy shield of plated armour covered its entire huge body, except for its underbelly and short legs. It seemed to be searching for soft vegetation on the ancient floodplain floor, digging with its hooves for tuberous roots in the moist earth.

Mildred whispered excitedly in Daniel's ear over the gentle snuffling and snorting of the creature. "This is the first proof that *Ankylosaurs* ever lived in Saskatchewan! I was sure they had."

Daniel nodded; he'd seen them on his last trip. But as far as research went, the remains of this plant-eater had only been found in Montana, Wyoming, and Alberta.

"Will you look at that wide, thick skull," said Mildred, snapping pictures. "No wonder they had such tiny brains. There wasn't any room for them."

They stared at the creature, taking in its flat, triangular skull that was nearly one metre long and very broad and thick. Massive knobs and plates of bone were embedded in the skin along the back and sides of its entire body, which ended in a club-like tail made of bony tissue encased in tough reptilian skin.

Daniel was so intent on watching the *Ankylosaurus* grazing on low-lying plants that he hardly noticed the increased whirring and loud booming sounds around them until Mildred nudged him. He listened. Something like a foghorn on a boat sounded and then an answering call.

"I bet that's hadrosaurs," said Dr. Roost.

Daniel knew the only hadrosaur that had ever been found in the province was the *Edmontosaurus saskatchewanensis*, like Roxanne.

"We shouldn't be far from the female one with the eggs that I found before." He kept his voice low so as not to startle anything. "I think it could be Roxanne."

As they proceeded, small creatures skittered through the underbrush, avoiding them with little squeaks. Once Daniel narrowly missed stepping on a multicoloured snake. Oversized insects buzzed languidly in the freshness of the early morning. He wasn't sure if they would attack or not, so he found a small branch and waved it about in the air around him. Mildred used her cane, swatting with determination and keen interest.

Intermittently, the ground trembled beneath their feet. Some huge creature must be in the area. The tenseness in Daniel's body increased the farther they probed into the forest. Huge redwood trees obscured their view ahead in the still mounting dawn. On top of that, the foliage was so dense everywhere, they couldn't see very far in any direction. Daniel began seeing large, shadowy shapes that turned out to be clumps of thick fern or tight stands of trees. What he thought were oddly shaped branches and undergrowth turned out to be creatures. Perils surrounded them in all shapes and sizes – airborne and land-roving.

He was prepared to dart away and always kept a tree in sight that he could easily climb, but fretted about Mildred Roost. The best she'd be able to do was hide in some underbrush, but that would be of little use. She followed behind him at a surprisingly agile pace through the thick tangle of growth, although she breathed heavily and stopped often to snap photographs. Daniel took those opportunities to tie bits of tape on the bushes about every fifteen to twenty metres, ensuring they'd be able to follow their trail back.

"This is incredible," she spoke softly to Daniel. "I can't believe my good fortune in being here!"

"So far, so good," he answered, turning to look at her.

"Yes, I know we're not out of the woods yet." She laughed at her own joke.

Even without the heat of direct sun, her face was flushed and beads of sweat dotted her forehead, although she didn't complain. But Daniel could see the exertion of pushing through the thick foliage was taking its toll on her.

"Would you like to take a little break for some water?"

She nodded. Daniel found another huge cycad and they pushed under some large fronds, then each drew a bottle of water from their backpack. Mildred's eyes were alert as she looked around her.

"We'll be in an open meadow soon," Daniel explained. "We'll have to cross it to get to the *Edmontosaurus*."

"That means even more danger." Her lips tightened in concentration. "If something happens, Daniel..." she started to say.

But Daniel protested.

"No listen," she insisted. "I want you to save yourself."

Daniel looked at her in horror. "Don't even say it! I wouldn't leave you behind."

"You may not have a choice," she answered grimly. "And I won't be responsible for your not getting back."

Daniel shook his head passionately. "We're both going to get back!"

Deep down, though, he worried that neither one of them would see home again. Why had he ever let Dr.

Roost come with him? An old lady was still an old lady. He bet she couldn't even run. He heard her sigh and tuck her water bottle back into her pack. Daniel returned his too, and they set off again.

All of a sudden, loud snorting growls came from just ahead of them. The little hairs at the back of Daniel's neck stood on end. He halted and Mildred Roost nearly ran into him. He motioned with his finger against his lips for her to keep silent and move back along the trail. As quietly as they could, they pushed the vines and low-lying branches out of their way. Without knowing what it was, they'd have to circle around it. Daniel wasn't sure which way was the best to go. He'd have to climb a tree to get his bearings. But he didn't want to leave Dr. Roost on the ground.

He voiced his dilemma to her.

"You go ahead and climb," she said, patting her backpack. "I have a few tactics in mind. All we need is right in here."

"Was that why you took so long to pick up the plaster from town yesterday?" Daniel asked, suddenly realizing that Dr. Roost had known all along about his plans and had intended on coming with him. Her expression was one of innocence, but Daniel could tell by the twinkle in her eyes that he was right. There was no time to ask what she'd brought in preparation for the trip. The snorting was getting closer.

Quickly, Daniel found what looked like a secluded enough spot off the beaten trail, and picked out a suitable climbing tree. Then they searched for a good place for Mildred Roost to hide while she waited.

"There." She pointed to a snarl of fallen tree trunks covered with vines and rotting debris that had left enough space for her to crawl into.

"Let's check it out first," Daniel suggested, remembering some of the strange creatures he'd discovered on his other trips.

Dr. Roost poked her cane into the opening. Daniel shuddered at the thought of what she might be disturbing.

"I don't think you should do that," he said. What if it were a den for baby meat-eating dinosaurs?

Dr. Roost retrieved a flashlight and bent to take a look and declared it safe. "I'll be right here."

Daniel nodded and scrambled up the tree as quickly as he could. By the time he reached a good vantage point, he was breathing heavily. He dug out the binoculars and surveyed the scene below, following the path they'd just come down. His stomach became one balled knot as he saw the creature they'd almost run into. He had to get down to Dr. Roost as soon as he could. A *Troodon* was bounding their way.

Daniel slid halfway down the tree, but the close sounds of the *Troodons* crashing through the trees made him freeze.

"Dr. Roost," he called as loudly as he dared.

She poked her head out of the den of fallen logs. Quickly, he told her what was coming. She looked at him in horror, knowing that a *Troodon* would rip them apart in seconds.

"You'll have to get as far back in as you can," he said. "Quick!"

Mildred Roost ducked back into the hole, just as the *Troodon* made the last turn around a bush and skidded to a stop beneath Daniel's tree. Balancing itself with its tail, it slashed towards Daniel with its long, clawed fingers. Daniel scooted higher up the tree again as fast as he could, not daring to look down until he figured he was safe.

By then the creature's big, keen eyes had spotted Dr. Roost's hiding place. It sniffed around the opening, clawing at the dirt with its sickle-like toes. Then it tried to reach in with its claws on the end of its shorter arms.

Daniel had to do something! Dr. Roost must be terrified, and what if it managed to snag her and drag her out with its long powerful legs? Known to have a relatively large brain, the *Troodon* was thought to be very intelligent. Daniel was sure it knew something alive and worth eating was inside. It wouldn't give up easily.

Quickly, he swung his backpack around and rummaged through it. The whole scene was a like a déjà vu. Every time he came to the past, he ended up a tree with something attacking him from below! Aha! He grabbed a package with some sandwiches, and with as much force as he could, he threw one far down the path. The *Troodon* sprang after it and snatched it in a millisecond.

"Don't move a muscle, Dr. Roost. And don't answer me or it will know for sure you're in there," called Daniel, as the fast-moving meat-eater dashed back towards them. Hopping over to the tangle of branches where Mildred Roost hid, it attacked the brush like a giant, rabid wolf.

"I'm trying to think of something to distract it long enough so we can get you out of there," he yelled again, just as the *Troodon* leapt at the bottom of his tree trunk once more.

If only they were close together, Daniel could drop the cone and they'd be back home, safe. Somehow he had to get her out of there and they had to escape the *Troodon*.

CHAPTER NINE

Then Daniel remembered his whistle. Yanking it out, he blew on it shrilly several times. The creature paused in momentary confusion, but then let out an angry, high-pitched snarl and vaulted back over to Dr. Roost's hiding spot. It attacked the fallen debris with renewed vigour. As some of the brush began to fall away, he heard Dr. Roost scrabbling back as far as she could.

"Stay where you are!" Daniel yelled, knowing he had to come up with another plan quickly. "I'll tell you when to come out."

He repositioned himself and dug out more sandwiches. It was the only distraction he could think of.

"Get ready," Daniel yelled. Then, flinging several as far and as fast as he could in a wide arc, he prepared to scuttle down the tree.

The *Troodon* took the bait, diving after the sandwiches one after another as they lay scattered throughout the forest floor. The creature was fast, though, and Daniel knew he'd barely have time to get down before it returned. And then what? They'd both be stuck on the ground and he might not make it over to Dr. Roost's lair in time.

Then a surprising thing happened. Other smaller creatures darted out of the underbrush and snatched at the sandwiches. In turn, the *Troodon* pounced on the tiny animals, taking time to devour them in quick, snapping bites as if they were nibbles in a bowl of snacks.

"Now!" Daniel yelled.

With a swiftness that surprised Daniel, Dr. Roost emerged and wrestled herself to her feet with Daniel's help.

"We'll have to return to our own time," he said, reaching for the pine cone in his pocket.

"No!" she said. "We're just getting started." She might be an old lady, but Daniel saw the resolve on her weathered face.

"But you'll have to climb, Dr. Roost," he explained. "It's the only way."

"I can do it," she said, with determination. "But you should go home," she declared.

"No way! Besides you'd be stranded in dinosaur time!" Daniel insisted. "We'll be fine if we're in the trees."

"Then let's do it."

They ran to a huge tree with sturdy branches that would hold both of them. Dr. Roost hesitated for a second. Then she looked over her shoulder towards the sounds of something crashing through the brush.

"You don't need to go really high," he encouraged her. The *Troodon* wasn't much taller than an ostrich.

She dropped her cane against the trunk. Daniel cupped his hands, one under the other for strength. She gritted her teeth and stepped into them. A moment later, she grabbed onto a branch, and she hoisted herself up, as Daniel helped boost her into the tree. At first, she clung awkwardly, not moving.

"You have to go a *little* higher," he shouted, giving her bottom a hard shove.

She struggled, but managed to inch upwards. Daniel grasped a lower branch and swung himself up. Then he worked his way around the trunk onto some limbs just slightly above her and helped her get higher. Her plump arms had surprising strength in them, and within moments, she was wedged in the crook of a branch, her hat cockeyed, and her clothing askew. Her hair stood out like a scarecrow's with bits of twigs and leaves stuck in it. Daniel giggled quietly, both from her comical look and from a nervous reaction to fear. Dr. Roost laughed a little too, as she concentrated on staying put.

Daniel balanced himself on another branch nearby, keeping his eye on Dr. Roost. She wheezed and stared about. As she twisted her head this way and that, her Tilley hat caught on a branch and fell to the ground. In the same instant, the vicious creature erupted again from the undergrowth and pounced on it.

Dr. Roost shrieked.

In a split second her hat was in shreds. Daniel gulped and clung tighter to the tree trunk.

"That could have been one of us!" Dr. Roost panted, her face white.

They stared down as the sharp-clawed meat-eater leapt towards them, snarling fiercely. It scoured the ground at the base of the tree, moving between there and Dr. Roost's previous den. At one point, it sniffed at her cane and knocked it to the ground.

"*Zapsalis!*" Mildred Roost suddenly screeched.

"Pardon?" Daniel looked at her with surprise.

"I bet that's a *Zapsalis*," she said. "It's definitely from the Troodontid family, but smaller. We don't know too much about this animal, but for certain, it ate meat."

"I didn't think they lived around here," Daniel said.

"They found the teeth just across the border in Montana, so I guess they were here too – obviously," she answered with a nervous chuckle. "Never thought I'd see one quite this close."

Daniel wished they weren't this close either.

Dr. Roost struggled for her camera, nearly losing her balance. Soon she was snapping as many photos as she could of the *Zapsalis*. After quite some time, the creature gave up and finally wandered off. As Mildred Roost shot photos in every direction that she could see, Daniel surveyed the landscape, trying to decide which way to go.

On higher ground, he could see tall deciduous trees towering above the rushes that lined the various riverbanks. Then he noticed a stronger flow of water. As his eyes followed it, he saw that the mouth of the river connected with the giant shallow sea. This had to be the same river he'd seen the last time he been here – the one where the female *Edmontosaurus* nested.

"Uh, Dr. Roost," Daniel said at last. "I think it's safe to go now."

"Okay, young man," she said, tucking her camera away.

"Do you need some help?" Daniel asked, seeing her sudden look of terror.

"Maybe," she said tightly.

Daniel groaned inwardly.

"I've never rightly been up a tree before. Not sure I *can* get down."

"Dr. Roost!" Daniel couldn't hide his dismay.

"Don't worry, Daniel," she said, easing herself out of the crook of the tree and grasping a nearby bough. "I'm a believer in Newton's law of gravity."

With sudden realization, Daniel chuckled. "What goes up must come down."

She smiled, and then began the descent in earnest, grabbing at branches and muttering under her breath whenever she hit a snag or couldn't find her footing. Daniel slid down the other side of the tree quickly and waited at the bottom, helping her as best he could. Her bulky figure was too much for him to catch and she dropped that last few feet to the ground and rolled.

"Whew!" Dr. Roost said, struggling back to her feet. "That was quite an experience."

"Let's hope we don't have any more of them!" Daniel said, helping to brush her off and picking up her cane. She took it gratefully.

"Would you mind picking up my hat?" she asked. "I'm sure Ole will get a kick out of it."

Daniel retrieved the shredded hat, and she tucked it into a side pocket of her backpack. Then he crept forward, keeping a sharp lookout. Now that he knew in which the direction the river lay, he headed there. They wouldn't stop until they reached their main destination – the nesting *Edmontosaurus*. But they had to get a move on! Danger lurked everywhere. This wasn't some fossil field expedition where everything stood still and he had all the time in the world to investigate.

They pushed on through the undergrowth, weaving through dense bush and marshy areas, avoiding any places that seemed likely to be inhabited. There was little time for conversation and Dr. Roost ploughed valiantly along behind him for quite some time. Daniel thought they must be getting close to the meadow, but as he searched for an opening in the trees, he suddenly realized he was in unfamiliar territory.

The trees seemed larger and towered higher above them than anywhere else. Other plants and vines wound around the densely packed trees, reaching towards the sunlight. As Daniel and Mildred Roost went farther along, they found themselves under a canopy of vegetation that seemed dark and foreboding. The foliage formed an umbrella over them and blocked out the sun and the mist. He froze! Where were they?

"Something wrong, Daniel?" Dr. Roost asked, noticing his hesitation.

"I just need to check something." Dragging off his backpack, he dug out his hand-drawn map. Then he pulled his compass out of his pocket. As he studied his surroundings, he realized he was lost!

Mildred Roost peered over his shoulder. "So what's the prognosis?" she asked.

"We're a little off course," he managed to croak out. "We'll have to do some backtracking."

"You're sure, lad?" Dr. Roost asked, trying to keep her voice steady.

"Yes," Daniel answered, his own voice wavering slightly.

"Do you know where we went wrong?" she asked gently but firmly.

"I think so," he answered, looking carefully around.

All the plant life here looked more abnormally large than anything they'd previously encountered. The blossoms on the magnolia trees and the other bright flowers seemed magnified even from their normal prehistoric size. Daniel brushed against an oval-shaped plant with yellow leaves lying flat to the ground. The leaves immediately tried to curl around his foot. He jumped back. He looked more closely at the plants around them, noticing another plant covered with tiny, red hairs. A huge insect buzzed close by it, and was instantly stuck to it. Daniel froze.

"Don't move," he yelled.

Dr. Roost stopped in her tracks.

"These plants may be flesh-eating," he exclaimed.

Mildred Roost studied them without moving any part of her body except her head. She indicated the vine close to Daniel's feet. Was it his imagination, or was it snaking out towards him?

"Back out the way you came," Dr. Roost said, clutching her cane.

Daniel clasped his arms to his body and carefully backed out of the dense woods. He kept his eye pinned on the foliage, not sure what would try to grab him. He carefully avoided what looked like a giant Venus flytrap. He'd seen how quickly this plant, with its unusual bristled lobes, snapped shut on insects, and this one was so huge that he might become its next prey.

When he was safely out, Mildred Roost pulled out her camera and took a number of shots from different angles without taking a step. Daniel hoped there was enough light to have good photographs. This opportunity was too good to miss.

At last, Dr. Roost came out with her cane raised, prepared to hack if something threatened to engulf her. They didn't take the time to look at the photographs. When they considered themselves safe again, they stopped.

"Whew, I've never seen anything like that before," Daniel claimed.

"I don't know that we want to again, either," said Dr. Roost with an indignant chortle. "It's one thing to be gobbled by a prehistoric reptile that thinks you're nothing more than an annoying insect, but quite another for a plant to squeeze the life out of you."

Daniel started laughing nervously. "Yeah, being slowly absorbed by a plant doesn't make quite as good a story as being swallowed by a *T. rex*."

Dr. Roost chuckled. "No telling if they were poisonous or not. I decided we could do without samples for now!"

"At least you got some photos!"

"Good thing, otherwise no one would ever believe us! Not that many will anyway."

Serious once again, they consulted about how far they had to go to get back on the right trail. In order to get his bearings, Daniel scrabbled up the nearest tree, pushing vines out of the way, ignoring thoughts of people-eating plants. He cut his hands on sharp-edged leaves, and scraped his legs and arms on rough bark as he dragged himself upwards as fast and as high as he could go. Exhausted, he clung to a tiny branch near the top of the redwood tree. The sweat ran down his forehead and his face stung where it seeped into open scratches. The treetop swayed with his weight.

All at once, he caught a glimpse of the river and could see the path to their right where they'd veered in the wrong direction. Mentally, he imprinted the information and joined Mildred Roost back on the ground, sure that he knew the route to take.

Not long afterwards they found their way, following the strips of tape Daniel had tied along their path. He made sure to take away those that led to the weird carnivorous plants. He never wanted to go there again. As they pushed onwards, the fresh smell of pine and the sweetness of magnolia blossoms were keen in the pure air untouched by modern pollution. Several times they nearly tripped on roots and scrubby brush, startling little lizard-like things that flicked into previously unseen holes.

A short time later, they came to the marshy meadow. The temperature had risen, and so had the humidity. Tying a piece of tape to a tree on the edge of the open area, Daniel decided they would need to drag some branches with them to mark the way across. Quickly, he dug out his Swiss Army knife and cut several lengths, handing them to Dr. Roost.

"Maybe just a few more," she suggested, clutching them in her arms. "We want to make sure we find our way back."

Daniel loaded her up, then put away his knife and took the bundle from her. Every few hundred metres, they stopped and Daniel constructed a teepee shape tied with tape, until the markers stretched in a wavering line behind them that they could easily see.

At times, they almost sank to their ankles in sticky black ooze when they came through a particularly low spot. Mostly, they were on solid but rough ground. Camouflaged beetles and unfamiliar gopher-sized mammals with beaky noses darted about, criss-crossing their path in the long grass and reeds. Once they came upon a string of marsupials – odd-shaped opossum-like creatures.

"In all my days in paleontology, I never expected to see such cute but odd-looking creatures!" Dr. Roost lifted her camera to take more shots. "I wish Ole could see this."

"So how long have you been doing paleontology work?" asked Daniel, suddenly curious.

"As far back as I can remember," she shrugged her shoulders. "Even when I was younger than you, I knew what I wanted to do. Guess it helped that we lived near the hoodoos in Alberta."

"Awesome!"

"Indeed, we went there on school trips often when I was going to high school, but I'd beg my parents to take me to the badlands any chance I could. I couldn't get enough of it. I volunteered to work at the Alberta dinosaur park during the summers after it opened in 1955. I had some good guidance and eventually went on to study paleontology formally." She stopped for breath and smiled. "Guess that doesn't rightly answer your question about how long I've been doing it, but I'm not about to tell you my age!"

"That's okay! You don't have to tell me." Daniel laughed. "So how long have you known Mr. Pederson?"

"My, you are inquisitive." Mildred Roost grinned. "We met as undergrads at the University of Alberta, but I went away to graduate school and he stayed behind."

"But you kept in touch?" asked Daniel.

"Off and on. We met from time to time at various paleontological dig sites, but by then we were both married to other people, and over the years I kind of lost track of him. But I'd never forgotten him."

They pressed on into the middle of the clearing, wondering if they'd ever get to the other side. Whenever the trail allowed, Dr. Roost stayed close beside him, not speaking a word, nor taking many pictures. He knew she scoured the area as intently as he did, both making sure nothing was sneaking up on them, including from behind or above. They could certainly see something coming from a long distance away, but there really wasn't anywhere for them to hide.

Mildred Roost pushed on without any complaint, although Daniel could see she struggled to keep up with him. He didn't know what he'd do if she couldn't go on or was injured somehow. So far they'd managed, but what lay ahead? Fear spurred them on, but Daniel was tense the whole time until they'd crossed the meadow, their feet squishing in their sodden shoes.

Finally they reached the other side and found cover in the trees. Daniel stopped momentarily so he could catch his breath. He knew Dr. Roost needed a break. She whipped a handkerchief out of her pocket and wiped her brow.

"Whew," she said. "That wasn't much fun."

Daniel agreed, but they had to keep moving. They must be close to their destination. Although his stomach rumbled with hunger, they couldn't stop to eat yet. The sooner they got where they were going, the sooner they could return home. Besides, he'd thrown all of the sandwiches to the *Troodon*, so all they had were the granola bars.

They took quick drinks of water, while he tied another marker, and then they entered dense trees again. The stands were so tall and overbearing and their girth so wide that Daniel soon became confused about direction. Although he used his compass, he wanted to see where he was headed. Once again, he climbed a tree to determine their position, while Dr. Roost waited patiently below.

As Daniel began to descend, he saw a fifteen-centimetre spider scrambling up the trunk towards him. Its beady scarlet eyes and tentacle-like hairy legs were scary enough, but its long pointy beak looked like it could drill a hole right into his leg.

He tried to kick at it, but it seemed to be glued to the bark. He needed something to pry it off with. One eye on the spider, he dug around in his backpack, but there was nothing. In a blur of legs, the spider suddenly moved much closer. In a panic, Daniel reached up to another branch, hoping to climb away.

The branch felt all wrong.

Daniel screamed. It was a snake! He let go and clutched the branch below him. He was caught between the two-metre, boa-like reptile and the furry spider. He was too high to jump to the ground. Either one could come at him any second. He saw the spider start towards him, but the snake was faster. He drew in his breath it as slithered downwards past him and snapped up the spider, swallowing it whole.

Daniel hoped the serpent would disappear. It did at last, continuing down the tree until it reached the ground and vanished into the undergrowth.

CHAPTER TEN

When they reached the edge of another smaller open area, Daniel stopped short. Dr. Roost almost bumped into him. Two creatures, each about the size of a full-length car, although they weren't much taller than Daniel, confronted one another. They reminded him of bighorn sheep with their enormous domed heads. Their skulls were bumpy and they had a ring of bony knobs at the base around the neck and towards the small eyes. Short, bony spikes protruded upwards from the back of their heads.

Suddenly, Daniel's mouth dropped open when he realized what he was seeing.

"*Stygimoloch*," he whispered.

Dr. Roost whispered back. "They look different from what I expected. They're even fiercer looking than any drawings, especially their heads."

Suddenly, the pair of *Stygimolochs* stood on their hind legs. They each let out a booming low call, like a foghorn on a ship.

"That's what we heard before," Daniel realized.

Mildred Roost nodded.

"Could I have the camera?" Daniel asked when the massive creatures didn't appear to notice them.

Dr. Roost handed it to Daniel wordlessly. He took several shots as the two animals circled one another, and then another couple when they began clashing heads. They made tremendous clunking noises each time their armour-like skulls connected. Daniel skirted them with care.

"Don't go any closer," Dr. Roost warned, treading softly behind him.

"No way," he agreed, sticking the camera away within easy access. Then he tied a piece of tape on a tree branch and they set off again. Daniel eyed the creatures warily until they were out of sight.

They continued to hear the foghorn sounds after they'd left the pair of discontented creatures. Not long afterwards, they came across a small herd of about ten hadrosaurs under a grove of pine trees. Daniel recognized them right away as *Edmontosaurus saskatchewanensis*. They were gathered loosely together, foraging for food. Some concentrated on higher pine needles, while the smaller ones feasted on cones and twigs. Their nesting grounds must be nearby! Maybe he and Mildred Roost were getting closer to the injured female.

Daniel quickened their pace. They circled the meadow and the herd. Even though these dinosaurs were plant-eaters, he wasn't sure what they'd do in order to protect themselves and their young if they saw humans or smelled human scent. They were huge beasts, and one stomp from them would end his or Dr. Roost's life in seconds. He did take several snapshots of them, though, from different angles, and Dr. Roost jotted notes in a journal. Daniel also made sure to take time to mark the places they passed.

Soon the air became moister and breathing became more difficult. Dr. Roost wheezed behind Daniel, but wouldn't let him stop. He could feel himself tiring. All of the terrain looked the same, and he couldn't recall any distinguishing features. Then he noticed gull-like creatures wheeling into the sky in the distance. They must be flying over the river! They had to be near the injured female! He hurried forward, and Dr. Roost sensed his excitement and moved faster as well.

"Are we almost there?" she asked, puffing slightly.

"Yes," Daniel said confidently. He wasn't going to admit to Mildred Roost that all he could remember was that the *Edmontosaurus* was sheltered under an over-hanging bank beside the river.

Finally, as they struggled through some particularly dense foliage, they emerged into a clearing. The water's edge was just ahead. Daniel followed the river's twists and turns for several hundred metres, hoping they'd stumble upon the duckbill nest without further endangering the crusty old doctor or himself. They scuffled unevenly through the silt on the shore, stopping every once in a while to shake the dirt out of their shoes.

All at once, they rounded a bend in the river, and there she was!

Daniel and Dr. Roost crept towards the nest. She had already commandeered the camera and was snapping shots. Daniel kept watch for predators. He didn't want to be caught off guard, but it was hard to concentrate when the goal of his trip lay just ahead.

When they got closer, they saw that the mother *Edmontosaurus* lay encircled around her nest, guarding her eggs as best as she could. Her leathery sides heaved as she tried to take in air, the large pouches by her nose expanding with each breath. Her huge golden eyes barely opened as they approached. She had little strength left and gave only a weak snort.

"Is that the same *Edmontosaurus* you saw before?" Dr. Roost asked.

"Yes, I'm positive it is," Daniel answered.

"This is an amazing opportunity to see one up close."

Mildred Roost crept nearer, seeming not the least concerned for her own safety. Daniel moved to pull her back, but soon realized that although the *Edmontosaurus* seemed aware that they were there, she could do nothing about it and they were relatively safe. Mildred took more close-up photographs as Daniel moved in to study the *Edmontosaurus*, looking for evidence that she might be Roxanne, the same one that he and Mr. Pederson had excavated in the present.

As he circled her body, he saw again the unnatural angle of her left hindquarter. The injury was obviously serious enough to inhibit activity. He moved around her until he stood where he could reach her forearms with their mitten-like hands. The top one was tucked tightly against her chest, while the bottom one flopped outward onto the ground. From the angle of it, Daniel was positive it was broken too.

Both breaks seemed to coincide with those on the fossil they'd found, but there were other characteristics he needed to research before making a more positive identification. Roxanne's fossil had been surrounded by little babies, but this one only had eggs that were beginning to crack. He couldn't see anything wrong with her head, either, as the photos from the RSM had shown. He had no way of knowing what would happen to this one when she died or how or if she would be preserved. The *Edmontosaurus* that he and Mr. Pederson had found seemed to have been buried along the riverbank, which was a strong similarity but not conclusive.

Daniel's thoughts turned again to how amazingly different the creatures in this world were from his own. He couldn't fathom how the prehistoric ones had evolved or vanished and present-day animals had appeared. Yet they had, and whether wild or not, they were still living creatures.

As he watched the suffering creature, Daniel wished he could do something. Maybe he could feed her? As quickly as he could, he climbed the embankment.

"Where are you going, Daniel?" Mildred Roost asked a little anxiously.

As he explained his mission, she nodded. "I guess I don't need to tell you to be careful?"

A few metres away, there was a copse of pine trees. Scouring the surroundings, Daniel hurried over to them and grabbed a handful of pine cones and twigs lying on the ground. He wasn't sure if she would eat it, but all he could do was try. Returning to the mother dinosaur, he placed the food on the ground right by her mouth.

She gave a short, snorting sniff, but didn't have the strength to reach for the food with her enormous tongue. Daniel decided that there was no way he was going to hand-feed her the way he did his horse Gypsy! Her flat-beaked head was humungous, and even if he could have lifted it off the ground, he wasn't getting that close to the hundreds of closely packed teeth in her cheeks. Herbivore or not, he was sure she could crush his hands!

Even if he dared to feed her and she did eat something, how much would she need? And for how long? There was no way he could stay here for days on end to take care of her. Her breaks would probably never heal. The bird-like carnivores circling overhead seemed to know there was not much hope for her as they gave a long screeching call, like the caw of a crow, to one another.

Suddenly, Daniel noticed several tiny hatchlings partway out of their shells. No movement or noise came from any of the other dozen or so eggs. Daniel gulped back the sadness making his throat ache. He knew it would only be a short time before the *Edmontosaurus* died. But he tried one more time to feed her, realizing that she wasn't going to bite him.

He even tried to open up the top part of her beak to set some food inside her mouth. As he did so, she gave a slight jerk. Her head rose off the ground just long enough for Daniel to see the dried blood caked to it. So her head *was* injured too. One more reason to believe that maybe this was Roxanne!

Daniel moved in closer and gently touched her tough skin. It felt like old leather, rough and thick. Feeling braver, he stroked her neck and nose the way he did his horse Gypsy. He wondered if she could even feel his hands running over her tough thick body. Her heaving breaths were intermittent and laboured. After a while, she didn't even bother to open her eyes.

Feeling fairly safe beside her, Daniel sat down and recorded his findings, making notes about her condition and the special features of her body. Mildred Roost continued to take detailed photographs.

After a time, Daniel could no longer ignore the rumblings in his stomach. He realized he was getting weak from hunger.

Dr. Roost came over to him. "Time for a snack?"

"I sure could eat a sandwich right about now," he said. "Too bad the *Zapsalis* ate them all!"

"Not quite," she said with a smile, as she unzipped her backpack and drew out a couple of Baggies.

"Ham and cheese, my favourite!" said Daniel,

smiling and reaching for one without a moment's hesitation.

He gobbled a couple of sandwiches as he wrote in his journal, then swished them down with bottled water. He offered Dr. Roost an energy bar, but she declined and he wolfed two of them down too.

They sat back for a few moments, lost in their own thoughts. Daniel tried to estimate the time it would take to get to the spot to get back home. What if Dr. Roost couldn't make it? Maybe there was a shorter way, but he doubted it. Dr. Roost seemed very resourceful, maybe she could think of something. He was just about to ask her, when she spoke.

"You know, Daniel, you remind me of my oldest son," she said. "Always looking for adventure and usually finding it too."

"I didn't know you had a family!"

"Oh yes, two boys. My husband died eighteen years ago…a heart attack took him. He was a paleontologist too."

"Where are your sons now?" Daniel asked curiously.

"Randall, my youngest, lives in Vancouver with his wife and two daughters. He's a medical doctor," she answered. "He decided to help those living in the present."

She grew quiet for a moment, then said briskly, "And Trevor, I lost him in an avalanche on his way up to do some environmental studies at the North Pole."

Daniel was speechless for a few moments.

"I'm so sorry," he said finally.

She shrugged, although her eyes filled with sadness. "He was a good lad, doing what he loved to do. Geophysical research."

"How old was he? What was he doing? I mean, I know it's none of my business, but…"

She patted Daniel's arm. "He was thirty-four. He was part of a small group of scientists studying how climatic change at the North Pole might affect the global climate. He was particularly interested in researching how global warming is impacting on the world's atmosphere, oceans, and land masses."

"Wow, that's really important stuff!"

Dr. Roost gave a small chuckle. "Indeed. But the irony is that neither of my sons wanted to follow in their father's or my footsteps. Yet Trevor ended up working on almost exactly the kind of thing we're doing right now."

"How did that happen?"

"Over the years, there was growing evidence that the polar caps were actually warm during the Cretaceous Period. They've found fossils to prove it, like leaf fossils, mosasaurs, plesiosaurs, dinosaurs, marsupials, and champsosaurs. They actually believe there was global warming way back then."

Daniel turned this information over in his mind. How astounding.

Dr. Roost laughed again. "I used to tease Trevor about him ending up like his folks after all, but he'd just brush me off and grin. Then he'd proceed to tell me all about the latest fossils they found."

"You must really miss him," Daniel said.

"Yes, I do. It was a few years ago now, but I still miss our conversations." Mildred Roost turned to Daniel. "Like I said, you're a lot like him."

"Didn't he have any family?"

"Yes, I have a grandson, though he's a bit younger than you. I'm sure he'll make a good paleontologist some day, if I have any say in his upbringing. I'd like him to meet you some day, Daniel. You'd be a good influence for him. He could learn a great deal from you."

Daniel smiled with pride, not knowing what to say. No one had ever given him such a generous compliment before.

"Well, enough of this maudlin stuff." Dr. Roost stood up and brushed off her pants. "Time to get some more work done."

Daniel and Mildred Roost simultaneously pulled out their tape measures.

"Great minds think alike," said Dr. Roost, giving Daniel a thump on the back.

Gently, they measured the *Edmontosaurus*, including the circumference of her head, her eyes, her forearms, and her hind legs. All the while she lay docilely, almost as if they didn't exist. The tail was the hardest to measure with its series of bumps that ran all the way up her back and neck. He wasn't quite sure how far from the long pointed tip he needed to measure up her back. He sketched the dinosaur and marked her dimensions, figuring that this duckbill was at least thirteen metres long in total.

Her three-toed, hoofed feet were the most interesting to measure. Daniel plucked apart her toes, keeping a wary eye on her, in case she flicked him away. He would be seriously hurt if she did. And all the while he worked, he felt how incredible it was to be here with a real dinosaur, in a world others could only dream of.

Picking up the camera, Daniel took a sequence of photos showing the comparison of a small ruler to her teeth and other parts of her anatomy. While Dr. Roost lifted debris from the nest, he snapped details of the underside of the *Edmontosaurus*, the eggs, and her lifeless hatchlings. There would never be another opportunity like it!

Just as he got to his knees, he saw a sudden movement out of the corner of his eye. He realized that what he thought was a fallen log a couple of metres away, wasn't. Scrambling to his feet, he motioned to Dr. Roost and together they backed away as the two-and-a-half-metre, dark grey *Borealosuchus* slid into the water. Whew! They'd been so immersed in their research that they'd forgotten to watch out for predators.

Once the *Borealosuchus* had drifted downstream, Daniel moved to the water's edge and filled a vial. Water insects hovered around him. He tried scooping them into the vials, but that proved unsuccessful. He thought about catching them with his bare hands, but decided against it.

Moving back to Dr. Roost, he took another compass reading and studied the landscape, noting as many details as possible. Dr. Roost was packing up her gear, and she motioned to Daniel that she was ready to leave. He quickly stored away his stuff too.

As they were leaving the dying *Edmontosaurus*, Daniel stood over her for a few moments. A lump rose in his throat, as he gave her a farewell pat. Then they climbed up the embankment to the pine tree grove.

"Well, young man," Dr. Roost said, "this has certainly been an extraordinary experience."

Daniel nodded. "Now you can see why I had to come."

"Indeed," she said. "Thank you for bringing me along."

"Too bad we have to go back now," said Daniel.

"Oh, I think we could take a couple more minutes. I'd like to collect some plant samples yet."

Daniel grinned. "Great!" That was exactly his thought. And although he knew that they were collecting samples for scientific study, he couldn't forget something else about them. Each one could open a portal back to this exciting world.

CHAPTER ELEVEN

They took turns. One was the lookout while the other gathered specimens, storing them in Dr. Roost's bag. When it was Daniel's turn, he took out his Swiss Army knife, and carved off a small branch at its tip and put it into a plastic Baggie. Then he collected a leaf from an unusual looking tree and pressed it between the pages of his journal.

Slowly the increased sounds of forest life penetrated Daniel's consciousness. The sun had risen totally, casting a yellowish haze over their surroundings. It was getting later in the morning. He walked over to Dr. Roost and touched her shoulder.

"We'll have to get back home," he said, pointing to the position of the sun.

Dr. Roost sighed and pushed herself up off her knees.

Daniel walked over to a stand of redwoods. He found one of the tallest ones on the edge, and climbed it to get his bearings. Pulling out his binoculars, he gulped when he saw all the different species that surrounded him as far as he could see. More creatures were now awake and mobile.

Several small herds of herbivores grazed comfortably together in their chosen areas: *Stegoceras*, *Ankylosaurus*, *Stygimoloch*, *Triceratops*, and *Edmontosaurus*, and others Daniel didn't recognize. Various other rodent and mammal-like animals criss-crossed their paths, while flying creatures and insects filled the air. The forest was alive with eerie sounds.

Although he'd never been to Africa, Daniel had seen plenty of documentaries on the environment and was always amazed at the different species that fed in the same areas, oblivious to one another unless there was a predator amongst them. These creatures were doing the same thing, though they looked even stranger than those that roamed the Serengeti. Or were they?

If people had lived during the Cretaceous Period and had a chance to see the earth as it was now, what would they think of hyenas, rhinoceros, gazelles, zebras, giraffes, elephants, hippos, and wildebeests? The present world was full of weird creatures like primates, penguins, kangaroos, octopuses, and armadillos. The more he thought about all the creatures on earth today, the more he realized that everyone accepted them, but they were every bit as strange as those in the world of dinosaurs. Their existence depended on their habitat and the environment, just as it did in the prehistoric world.

Daniel stared through the binoculars again. The group of *Edmontosaurus* had moved on to another patch of trees. Daniel almost yelled as if to warn them of danger when he saw a small group of *Zapsalis* feeding on a rotting carcass only a few hundred metres away.

Dr. Roost noticed his agitation. "What's happening?" she asked.

He explained how close the *Zapsalis* were to the group of *Edmontosaurus*.

"There's nothing you can do about the natural order of things," she said. "What else is going on?"

"Besides the herbivores we've already seen, there's something I think is a *Torosaurus*."

"A relative of the *Triceratops* – known as the 'bull lizard,'" said Dr. Roost.

"The frilled neck crest is a little different, though," Daniel reported. "The plate is enormous and long, almost oval. It has the largest skull I've ever seen, with two brow horns and a short nose horn."

"Can you get any photographs?"

"I'll try, but they're kind of far away," replied Daniel.

Daniel handed over the binoculars to Dr. Roost and took the camera as the *Torosaurus* bit off small branches and tough vegetation with its strong beak. It stood on powerful legs that were short at the front and longer at the back, giving it a very stable posture.

"I think you can maybe just see them through those trees," he pointed the way out to her.

"Incredible!" she said. "Do you know how special this is to see all of these creatures?" Dr. Roost sounded overwhelmed. The expression on her face was one of complete awe and reverence.

"Oh, I think I see a herd of *Corythosaurus*-like dinosaurs. Here, take a look." She handed the binoculars back up to Daniel in exchange for the camera.

"They're dining on palm leaves, pine needles, fruits, and seeds." Daniel described them for Dr. Roost. "And then there is some kind of duckbill, similar to *Edmontosaurus* but smaller, heading towards the sea."

As he relayed the information, Mildred Roost jotted it into her special spiral-bound notebook. Daniel stopped at one point and dug out his dinosaur research book. He started comparing the species he didn't know to the descriptions in his book. Many of them weren't mentioned. Was that because they hadn't been discovered yet or just that he wasn't aware of them? He soon tucked the book away in frustration, realizing that his book was useless.

"Problems?" asked Dr. Roost.

"Some of these creatures aren't in the book yet."

Dr. Roost laughed. "That's not a bad thing. That probably means they haven't been discovered in the present world yet. We're the first to see them," she said excitedly, handing the camera back up to him. "Snap away and I'll write as fast as I can while you describe them."

They saw everything from small mammals and reptiles, to insects, and rodent and bird-like creatures. He hardly knew what to concentrate on first. They were all strange to his eyes and utterly fascinating in their shapes and colours.

"Chop, chop!" Dr. Roost said, waving her notebook. "We don't have much time, so start anywhere."

Daniel stared at the ground. Some distance away, a small raccoon-sized animal leapt about, chasing flying insects. An animal about the size and shape of a small pig, but with the armour of an armadillo and a short stubby tail like a Manx cat, pushed its long snout into the tuberous roots farther along a trail. Daniel had no idea what it might be, but described it as accurately as he could, while Dr. Roost made notations in her scribbler.

Then he watched fascinated as a group of leathery, hound-like animals ran down the trail like a pack of large wolves, sniffing at various spots. Although they ran on all fours, they were some kind of reptile with short front feet and a strong pointy tail. They stopped to rout out rodent-looking animals, and with one snap swallowed them. Directly below him, a rat-sized *Purgatorius* rummaged in the undergrowth. Other small mammal-type animals darted about.

"Wow! There is so much to learn about the Cretaceous Period yet," Daniel exclaimed as he watched all the unidentified creatures. "But there's no way we can record them all." That would take many trips over many years.

"You're right, Daniel," said Dr. Roost. "But we've already collected hundreds of times more information today than paleontologists have ever known before."

"Maybe we could make lists of the various categories?" suggested Daniel.

Dr. Roost disagreed. "I don't think there's time for that. Just take photographs as quickly as you can."

"Okay!" Daniel called down.

Dr. Roost frantically scribbled descriptive notes about each entry while Daniel captured all the creatures that he saw, thankful that they had a digital camera. He became so intent on looking downwards that he forgot to look up until a wave of air fluffed his hair and brushed his face. Fierce crimson eyes stared into his. Then with a flap of its three-metre wingspread, a *Pteranodon* swept upwards and circled back towards him. Terror gripped Daniel, constricting his throat so he couldn't breathe for several seconds.

"Dr. Roost," he yelled when he caught his breath. "*Pteranodon*! Make yourself as small as you can under that cycad."

As Mildred Roost scooted to obey, Daniel crammed the digital camera into his backpack and searched for a place to elude his predator. Scrambling upwards into some thicker branches, he tucked himself tightly against the trunk of the tree under a dense cover of leaves.

The *Pteranodon* swooped by his perch, sending a cascade of twigs and leaves fluttering to the ground. It made a wider loop, scanning for him, but it obviously couldn't see him, and with a disgusted screech it sailed away. Daniel leaned against a thick branch in relief, watching it disappear. The thing was the size of a small glider plane.

"It's all right to come out now," he called to Dr. Roost, not sure where she was.

At last he spotted her some metres off where she'd dived under a giant fern. She waved to him.

"I can hardly believe it's a *Pteranodon!*" she yelled. "I thought they died out twenty million years earlier."

"Maybe it's just from the same family," Daniel called out.

Dr. Roost nodded and began sketching something in her notepad.

Then Daniel saw the *Pteranodon* suddenly circle back and aim for him again.

"Hide! It's coming back!" Daniel hollered, clinging tightly to the tree.

Several huge wing flaps and all of a sudden the *Pteranodon's* menacing curved jaw pointed straight at him. But this time, with a sudden swerve, it came at him with its deadly clawed feet, snatching at him. In the last second, it veered to miss some branches, but Daniel felt a gust of air and the scratch of its leathery wing membrane against his cheek. He hardly had time to recover before it swooped again. He ducked around a limb just in time.

The third time it came at him, Daniel's grip slipped. The horrible reptile dove at him again, plucking him out of the tree by a strap on his backpack. Daniel flung himself wildly about and the *Pteranodon* lost its grasp. He tumbled hard to the ground.

He scrambled to his feet and raced for cover. He could hear the wings flapping as he ran. But he was too far from the safely of the cycads. The *Pterenodon* lunged at him. Daniel screamed and hit the ground rolling. In a moment it would have him.

Then he heard Dr. Roost screeching at the top of her lungs, and then some fierce sounds of thwacking. He rolled over and sat up just as Mildred Roost charged again and pummelled the creature's long beak with her cane. Disoriented from the unexpected attack, the reptile flapped its heavy wings and disappeared into the sky.

"Take that you flea-bitten reptile!!!" Dr. Roost shook her cane, breathing hard. "Daniel, are you hurt?" she called out, not taking her eyes from the sky.

"I'm okay," said Daniel sitting upright and staring at Dr. Roost in shock.

Her eyes were big and dark and round. Her hair, loose from its braid, stuck out in all directions. Leaves and bits of dirt and other vegetation clung to her shirt and pants. She looked like a ragged mountain lion ready to pounce.

When Dr. Roost seemed sure the *Pteranodon* was gone for good, she rushed over to Daniel's side and helped him to his feet.

"Are you all right?" she asked again.

Daniel nodded and took a few deep breaths, shaken from the ordeal, but glad to be safe.

"Well, that certainly got my heart pumping!" exclaimed Dr. Roost, as she composed herself somewhat and straightened out her dishevelled clothes.

Daniel found his voice. "Thank you," he said. "I think you saved my life."

"I thought *Pteranodons* were supposed to eat fish and such," she grumbled.

"I guess this one was more adventurous," he said, trembling.

"I'll say!" Dr. Roost took out a handkerchief and wiped her perspiring face. "We'd better get back right away, before something worse happens."

"Yeah, we've had enough for one day." Daniel said.

Suddenly, he heard loud crashing and horrific roaring reverberating through the forest.

"Not again!" Daniel wailed.

"What's happening?"

"You'd better take cover. I have to climb up again to see."

This time Daniel chose a different tree and shinnied up as quickly as he could. He dug out the binoculars and discovered a pair of *Tyrannosaurus rex* attacking one another near the edge of the woods.

"What is it?" Dr. Roost called from the base of Daniel's tree. She hadn't moved.

"*T. rexes* fighting!" Daniel hollered. "Don't move and you'll be safe where you are. They're shifting away from us."

Daniel watched as their huge tails whipped around, smacking into trees and each other. They wrestled onto the ground, flipping this way and that as their huge mouths and sickle-like claws ripped at one another's bodies. Furious bellows sent bird-like creatures into the skies, and the whole forest seemed to move with scurrying creatures fleeing the battle.

Daniel was embedded on his branch, watching the shocking scene, thankful that they were several hundred metres away. Even so, the ground trembled with the flailing, gruesome bodies. They crushed everything in their path. Neither would give in. This was a fight to the death.

"Tell me what's happening!" demanded Dr. Roost, assuming an attack stance, her cane ready to thwack something again.

Daniel reassured her that they were safe, and gave her a quick description of the action, as the pair of vicious beasts shifted towards the riverbank. Closer and closer they moved to the edge, twisting and thrashing. They clobbered one another with sharp lashings of their tails, snarled and tore at each other's heads. They were one massive ball of deadly giant lizard, rolling towards the edge of the embankment.

"Oh no!" Daniel shouted.

"What?" asked Mildred Roost, preparing to climb the tree.

"I think they're above the *Edmontosaurus* mother and her nest!"

He watched in horror as the bank collapsed and the two enormous snarling *T. rexes* plummeted over the edge.

Daniel and Dr. Roost kept still. They could still hear horrible screams and growls, then some splashing. From the tree, Daniel saw an occasional thrash of a tail farther along the riverbed. A horrendous roar sounded. Then, instant silence. The fight must be over.

One *T. rex* must be dead.

Daniel slumped against the branch. He let out a deep breath, tried to let his body relax. The *Edmontosaurus* was surely dead too. Now he knew how she'd died and been preserved. The embankment had been pushed over on top of her and she had suffocated under the earth, along with her babies. Sadness overwhelmed him as he thought about her. He knew for certain now. This was Roxanne.

And yet… Maybe they'd somehow missed her. He had to find out. He noted the location of the sun, moving higher into the sky, and knew they had to get back home soon. He'd go as fast as he could. He shinnied down the tree.

"What's up?" asked Dr. Roost, seeing his excitement.

He explained his plan. Surprisingly, she agreed.

"I'll stay here and keep a lookout, but you must take this!" She rummaged through her backpack and pulled out some kind of a handgun with a long barrel.

"No way!" he said. "That wouldn't stop anything. Their skins are too tough."

"A real gun wouldn't be any use, Daniel, but this is a flare gun. It might slow them down or scare them enough so you could escape." She held out the gun. "I won't let you go alone, unless you take it."

"Okay," he agreed, tucking it into his backpack.

"Be quick, lad!" She raised her bottled water. Her face was filled with lines of tension and she obviously needed to rest.

Daniel kept a wary eye out, noticing that many of the creatures had hidden when the *T. rexes* began their dreadful fight. Now, as he walked, tentative movements rustled around him. There was no telling when some creature might dart into his path.

Within a couple of minutes, he reached the riverbank, and started to run. Then he stopped. He wasn't sure where the second *T. rex* had gone. What if it was still lurking on the beach? Daniel hugged the edge of the overhang, creeping forward and listening intently. The hot, moist air pressed against him, and he heard the eerie cries of the flying reptiles, but nothing close by.

Then he spotted the defeated *T. rex,* unresponsive on the beach, half in and half out of the water. Its huge, lifeless body lay twisted, its neck at an odd angle. Daniel descended to the riverbank, giving the lifeless *T. rex* a wide berth. The horrible smell and ripped-open flesh, the blood pouring onto the mud, was more than he wanted to be near. He hurried on, averting his eyes.

He rounded the bend and stopped. The collapsed bank lay straight ahead. A huge mound of earth had fallen directly onto the spot where the injured *Edmonto-*

saurus and her nest had lain. Daniel sagged onto the ground, tears stinging his eyes. He thought about taking a photograph, but he didn't have the heart to do it.

Seeing a living duckbill up close had been unbelievably alien to him. Being in the presence of dinosaurs was the most amazing and foreign experience he could imagine and he would never forget it. And he would never forget Roxanne and her nest. He knelt and stared at the huge mound of earth that covered her, remembered how he had tried to feed her.

He felt something nudge his ankle and turned to find one of the hatchlings beside his leg. As he reached out to touch it, the tiny creature brushed up closer. Daniel stroked it gently. He felt the thin, smooth skin, like his mom's leather purse, felt the bones through the skin, and its teeth like little pins. As he held it in his lap, the little duckbill scratched his hands like a playful kitten, but its claws were razor-sharp and Daniel soon put it on the ground.

It opened its mouth and gave high-pitched squawks. Maybe it was hungry? Daniel scrambled partway up the bank and snatched some pine cones and twigs. He broke them into tiny pieces and began feeding the hatchling. It snatched at the food and ate it quickly, looking around for more. Daniel gathered armloads, enough to leave it some for when he'd gone.

Then he got out the vial of water he'd collected earlier and gave the little hatchling a drink. Fashioning a dip in the mud, he lined it with a leftover plastic sandwich bag and filled it with water from the river. He knew it couldn't last long.

Sadness engulfed him. What would become of it? He couldn't stay and protect it, and it was too small to take care of itself. There were just too many predators for the hatchling, just as there were in his world for orphaned fawns and fox kits. But those animals were still in existence, while this incredibly different species was now gone forever.

Suddenly, Daniel realized that he'd left Dr. Roost alone too long. He started to move off, looking back one last time at the baby duckbill. Oh no! The little creature was following him. It probably thought he was its mother. What was he going to do? He grabbed clumps of grass with the roots and dirt attached and made a circular pen around the hatchling, enclosing the water source. It would have food and water for a short time. After that it would have to fend for itself.

He heard the shrilling of the whistle. Mildred must be in danger. A sudden roar farther around the curve of the river brought him instantly to his feet. Maybe the *T. rex* had returned? He ran to help Mildred.

CHAPTER TWELVE

Daniel backtracked, using huge ferns and small bushes for cover, jumping over snarled roots and pushing through long vines. He moved as fast as he could, praying that nothing dangerous prowled nearby.

A sudden loud racket in the bushes down the trail brought him to a halt. The sounds came louder, and closer. Whatever it was, it was between him and Mildred Roost. Daniel scrambled towards the tallest pine tree.

Gripped by fear, he instinctively wanted to drop the cone, but if he did, Dr. Roost would be left behind. Swiftly, he clambered up the tree and saw Dr. Roost waving to him with her cane. She held the whistle in her other hand. Her backpack leaned against the tree beside her.

"Hurry! We have to get home!" she called out, starting towards him.

"I'll get there as soon as I can!" Daniel yelled back, as more noises erupted nearby.

Abruptly, she stopped in mid-step. She stared upwards past him, and then mouthed something silently to Daniel as she pointed behind him. Then she dived for cover under a nearby cycad.

Daniel looked over his shoulder just as a huge head on a long, sturdy neck rose towards him. Glowing orange eyes stared at him and he felt its hot breath on his face. Daniel froze, eye to eye with an *Iguanodon*-like dinosaur. Not an actual *Iguanodon*, because they had lived mostly in Europe, in the earlier Cretaceous Period, but this creature had a similar tough, toothed beak, long toes, and a conical spike on each thumb. Its height reminded him of a giraffe, but its body was as along as a school bus.

Moments later, several more of the same creatures appeared. Standing on their thick, column-like back legs, they easily reached the top of the tree Daniel clung to. He cringed as the one nearest to him used its hands to gather leaves next to his head. Its middle three fingers were bound together by a plump pad of skin, and it curled its little finger over to grasp food. If only it didn't decide to taste him or nudge him out of the tree.

Daniel lost all sense of time, and of his body. But his immobility seemed to save him. The dinosaur nibbling at his tree moved off. Several of the others sniffed the air cautiously, and then began grazing. Daniel didn't dare call to Dr. Roost for fear they'd discover her. Somehow, though, they had to communicate and get back together so they could get home. She was only a few dozen metres away.

Suddenly, he noticed Dr. Roost creeping stealthily through the trees towards him.

"Stop!" he yelled.

"Just come down," she commanded. "I'll be okay."

Cautiously, he slipped down the tree, moving as quietly as he could. The stocky *Iguanodon*-like herbivores shuffled around the tree and he had to jam himself up against the trunk to keep one from crushing him. He glanced over towards Dr. Roost and motioned that he would join her. How, he wasn't sure. He'd have to distract the giant creatures.

As quietly as he could, he rummaged in his backpack, but before he could pull anything out, a shot reverberated through the air. Daniel screamed. When he looked over at Dr. Roost, he realized she held a second flare gun.

As a flare sailed into the herd, they scattered in panic. Their powerful legs pounded the ground, their hoof-like claws churned up the earth. Dust and debris swirled around the heaving bodies. It was all Daniel could do to keep from being trampled. He flattened himself against the pine tree, but it offered little protection.

Another flare whistled through the air towards him. Daniel sidestepped it and yelled, "Dr. Roost!"

He wasn't sure the second flare had helped. The herbivores seemed too panicked to move away.

"Over here!" He could barely hear her shouting over the clamour.

Then he saw her through a sudden break in the stampeding dinosaurs. She shot off another flare and marched towards him at a rapid pace, her cane swinging wildly, as many of the creatures scattered around and away from them. She began to run towards him, then suddenly, went down. Daniel saw her grasp her ankle and cry out. Dust and debris swirled around her.

He had to reach her and drop the pine cone. Otherwise, she could be killed! But how was he going to get through the charging herd? He still had his flare gun, but that only seemed to be making the herd stampede more.

"Get my backpack!" He heard her scream again.

He could see it a few metres away, miraculously still propped up against a tree. The *Iguanodon*-like relatives were still milling about in frenzy. He groped in his backpack. There was nothing else he could do but fire a flare and hope he could get through. He sent the missile whistling into the air and dodged through pounding feet. He shot two more. At last, he reached Mildred Roost's backpack. It brought him closer to her as well.

Quickly, he fumbled through the contents.

"Try the starter gun," she yelled over the pounding noise.

He found another smaller pistol in the bag. Without hesitation, Daniel grabbed it and fired it into the air several times in rapid succession. Momentarily, it stunned the dinosaur herd, but perhaps the sound was too much like thunder and they soon seemed to ignore it. He didn't even have a chance to run.

He fumbled through the bag, drawing out more objects. He found several small packages with a peculiar substance in them. He held them up, hoping Dr. Roost could see them. Maybe they could help somehow.

"Light them and throw them," she hollered, realizing what he held. "They're smoke bombs."

He lit one and prepared to run. He threw the bomb. It took a moment for it to work, but he made it a few metres forward. With the second, he crept a little further. By the third one, though, the giant herbivores weren't reacting. He was almost close enough to rescue Mildred Roost, but the dinosaurs were regrouping.

"Daniel!" she screamed over the din. "Go home! It's too dangerous for you to stay."

"No, I won't leave you!" Daniel yelled back. He'd like nothing better than to get out of prehistoric time, but how could he possibly abandon her? He probably wouldn't even be alive if she hadn't rescued him from the *Pteranodon*.

"Nothing is working! You have to go!" she insisted.

Suddenly, one of the giant creatures began advancing towards Dr. Roost. There was no time to lose. Daniel had to save her! He looked at the flare gun in his hand, but it was probably useless. There was only one flare left. What could he do with that?

And then, close to Dr. Roost, he noticed one of the teepee-like structures that he'd made to mark their path. What if he could hit it with the flare? Would it catch fire and distract the dinosaur? He had to try. But he only had one chance. The enormous creature had almost reached her.

Taking careful aim, Daniel fired and hit the branches. After a few terrible seconds, the marker burst into flame in front of the *Iguanodon*-like dinosaur. It squealed and veered away seconds before it would have trampled her.

Daniel raced to Dr. Roost's side. Throwing her backpack on the ground, he grabbed her hands, pulling her clear of the dangerous fray. Then he tried to help her to her feet.

"I don't think I can stand up," she said, grimacing as she made an attempt to rise. "My ankle may be sprained."

"Let's just get you back then!" said Daniel.

"Wait!" she shouted. "My backpack!"

Her eyes raked over the spot a couple of metres away where Daniel had dropped it, but there was too much dust and debris flying about amid the huge stump-like legs and flipping tails. There was no way they could retrieve it.

"We'll have to go without it!" Daniel screamed, as another massive herbivore brushed close by them.

Daniel cringed as it stomped on a small creature the size of a cat. He didn't need any more prompting. He felt for the cone in his pocket, breathing a sigh of relief when he located it. He glanced at the sky as he readjusted his backpack. The sun was almost overhead. They needed to get back immediately, but where they'd land, he didn't know.

He turned his attention to the cone clutched in his hand. As he tightened his fingers around it, he grabbed Dr. Roost's hand. He took one last look around and then looked at his companion.

Suddenly, she screamed. "Look out!"

Out of nowhere, a tail whipped Daniel into the air. He lost his grip on Mildred Roost's hand and felt the cone slipping from his fingers.

"Dr. Roost!!" he shrieked, knowing he was returning to his own time without her.

Then a sizzling blackness engulfed him.

CHAPTER THIRTEEN

"**D**r. Roost!" Daniel shrieked again. He had landed on a hillside, falling on his side, instinctively rolling into a ball.

"I think you can call me Mildred now," a voice said behind him.

He turned. Mildred Roost lay on the ground, her crumpled face white and stunned.

"I thought I'd lost you!" Daniel sputtered, crawling to her side.

"You almost did, young man!" She stayed where she was as she struggled to gain her composure, taking in deep breaths.

"What happened?" Daniel felt the blood pounding through his veins and his heart thumped loudly. The terror of almost leaving Dr. Roost behind sunk in and he couldn't stop trembling.

"I grabbed onto your shirt-tail," she said with an indignant snort.

Daniel bowed and let his forehead touch the ground, resting for a moment and letting the peacefulness surround him. "I have never been so happy to touch this earth."

"I'm definitely happy to be on our home turf," she said, lying there. "But I'd be even happier if I were standing on it."

She began to tussle with her cane and flare gun, her arms and legs flailing like a beetle on its back trying to right itself. Daniel rose and helped her to her feet. But as she stepped down onto solid grassland, her legs almost buckled. Daniel saved her from falling. She tried again to put some weight on her right foot, but quickly lifted it again. She leaned heavily on Daniel, until she could get her cane in the right position.

"We've got to get help for you!" Daniel peered around. He wasn't quite sure where they'd landed. He couldn't see the hideout or anyone about, although they were definitely back in his own time in the rolling hills of the valley.

Judging by the position of the sun, he guessed it was mid-morning and someone had probably missed them by now. He fumbled in his backpack and drew out his whistle.

"This ought to get them here, if they're close by."

He gave three long piercing whistles, the signal for distress that they'd decided to use for guiding the tourists. He listened for a few moments, but didn't hear an answering response. He blew again, and the high-pitched notes sliced through the air, halting all natural sounds.

"Did you hear anything?" he asked Mildred Roost, thinking there might have been a muted reply.

She shook her head, and he immediately blew as hard and as long he could, until he was out of breath. When the shrieking echoes in his ears stopped ringing, he listened again.

"There!" he announced triumphantly, as another three shrill sounds permeated the air in return. "They'll be here soon."

"I'm so glad we both made it back safely," said Mildred. "Especially, you! I'd never have forgiven myself if something had happened to you."

"I wouldn't have felt very good about leaving you behind either!" Daniel patted her arm.

"Whew, I'm exhausted though." She leaned heavily on Daniel. "I can tell you one thing for sure. I'll never take this good old world and where we live for granted again!"

"I second that," Daniel said.

He blew the whistle again, to give the rescuers a sense of direction. Moments later, two figures appeared on the crest of a hill in the distance to their left. As they drew closer, they could make out Craig Nelwin and Ole Pederson hurrying towards them.

"Are you two out of your minds?" Mr. Pederson fumed, reaching them with long strides. "You went back to the past again, didn't you?"

He grabbed Daniel by the shoulders as if to shake him. Instead, he hugged Daniel hard. When he released him, Craig stepped forward, the relief noticeable on his face.

"We thought you were gone forever!" Craig thumped Daniel on the back. "Good to have you back!"

Pederson reprimanded them. "I ought to take that cane and use it on you both! What a dangerous, foolish thing to do!"

Although Pederson clamped his lips tight together in disapproval, the relief at having them back again was evident in his eyes. Then he embraced Dr. Roost. She let out a little moan.

"Mildred, you're injured!" He took stock of her.

"Just a wee bit of a problem with my ankle," she reassured him.

"We've got to get you off that foot." He turned to Craig, puffing a little. "Come on, lad. Let's get them over to my cabin. It's not far from here."

Craig and Mr. Pederson went on either side of Dr. Roost, but Daniel intercepted the old man and locked hands with Craig to form a chair with their arms. Ole Pederson conceded and reached for her cane and Daniel's backpack. Dr. Roost rested her arms over the boys' shoulders and allowed them to carry her.

"What about you, Daniel?" asked Ole Pederson. "Are you hurt at all?

Daniel shook his head. "Nothing that a little rest won't cure."

"Well, we can see that you get that!"

As they set off, Daniel realized the dig was just back over the hills in the direction that Craig and Mr. Pederson had come from. The old paleontologist's cabin lay just over the next hill. He also noticed that the sun was almost directly overhead. They'd been gone for several hours. Had anyone else noticed their disappearance?

"How did it go with chores this morning?" Daniel asked Craig, fishing for information on the situation at home.

"Fine," Craig answered, as the struggled with the weight of Dr. Roost. "Although your dad wasn't happy that we were doing them ourselves."

Daniel held his breath waiting to hear if there was more.

"Your mom wasn't either, but at least she defended you. She understood how important spending time at your hideout was for you."

Daniel felt a pang of guilt at having told his mom a lie.

Then Craig snorted. "If she only knew! How could you do such a stupid thing?" he scolded. "If I'd known we were covering for you so you could go back to dinosaur time, I never would have agreed."

"And you, Mildred," Pederson focused on Dr. Roost, as they jostled down a hillside. "You intended on going all along," he accused her. "I thought we were supposed to stop Daniel from going."

"Did you really think we could stop this young man when he was so determined?" she answered.

"I suppose not." Pederson shook his head, obviously not pleased with the way things had gone.

"I decided it was better if I went with him than if he eluded us another time and went alone."

Pederson grumbled, but conceded, "At least you're both safe!"

Mildred Roost sighed. "Yes, we're certainly thankful for that."

"For sure!" Daniel agreed.

Not long afterwards they reached the dilapidated cabin. It was more like a weather-beaten wooden shack really, crammed into a gully as close as possible against the hillside. A long, narrow lean-to jutted out from the main shack and butted into the hill. A pile of excavation dirt was dumped about twenty yards away. Just beyond it was a little white cross where Pederson's dog Bear was buried. He had died of old age the winter before.

Daniel hadn't been here for ages, but as Pederson opened the rickety door that threatened to fall off its hinges, he smiled. Nothing much had changed. The air smelled of mustiness and of earth. He and Craig followed Mr. Pederson as they stumbled through the gloomy darkness into the simple one-room cabin. Dumping Daniel's backpack just inside the door, Mr. Pederson leaned Dr. Roost's cane against the wall, then helped Daniel and Craig to ease her into the only comfortable seat in the house – an old armchair, missing some of its stuffing.

"Definitely a bachelor's pad!" Dr. Roost observed.

She and Craig stared about in silence as their eyes adjusted to the dimness. The floor was old boards laid over mounds of packed dirt that took a sudden dip towards the far wall and then disappeared under the makeshift cot. A wood stove, cold now, stood in the middle of the room, its pipes contorting and rising through the rafters. Against one wall, a small wooden hutch, which served as a kitchen cupboard, leaned precariously.

Weathered boards served as shelves all along the length and height of one sidewall. Stacks of books and magazines filled the bottom racks. The top ones were lined with a myriad of jars, bottles, and tins in all shapes and sizes.

"An apothecary too!" Mildred observed.

"What does that mean?" asked Craig.

Mildred pointed to the labelled containers of dried plants, powders, crushed blossoms, dehydrated berries, and seeds in various shades of greens, browns, and yellows, all assembled neatly in alphabetical order. As Craig examined them, she explained that Pederson mixed his own concoctions for medications.

"Amateur only," Pederson grunted, as he opened a small door that led into the lean-to.

Moments later an engine started, and Daniel knew Pederson had switched on the generator for power. He returned and yanked on a chain. Instantly, one side of the cabin flooded with light to reveal a long, rough-hewn table covered with dinosaur bones and various samples of fossil imprints beneath the slanted ceiling of the shorter wall.

"Wow!" Craig instantly went over to examine the fossils.

While Pederson busied himself searching for a Tensor bandage, Daniel pulled up a wooden chair, which was missing a few rungs, beside Dr. Roost and collapsed on it.

"How are you feeling?" he asked quietly.

"I'll be fine, lad," she said, patting his hand. Then she smiled. "Didn't we just have the adventure of a lifetime?"

"I'll say," Daniel agreed, grinning.

"Let's hear about it, then," Mr. Pederson said, as he turned on the nearby lamp and sat down.

He gently removed Dr. Roost's shoe and sock, noticing the mud on them. "I think I can lend you a clean pair of socks," he said, slipping the one off her injured foot. "These are only good for the fire."

"Not on your life," Dr. Roost hooted. She grabbed it and tucked it into her pocket. "This is a specimen!"

Pederson grinned. "Sorry, I didn't even think about that."

He began winding an elastic bandage around her ankle. She grimaced as he tightened it, but didn't complain.

"Where should we begin?" she looked at Daniel, when Pederson finished and gently laid her swollen, bandaged ankle on a chair with a pillow on it.

"How about we just hit the highlights for now?" Daniel raised his eyebrows at her and she nodded. Neither of them really wanted to tell about all the danger they'd been in. "First, we'll tell you about finding the *Edmontosaurus*."

Craig pulled up another chair and joined them, as Daniel and Mildred relayed their findings about the mother dinosaur and the nest.

Pederson became extremely excited. "So would you say this was our Roxanne?"

"I'm positive," said Daniel.

"I agree," said Dr. Roost. "But you can take a look for yourself."

Daniel scooted over to his backpack and brought it to them. He fished out the camera and scanned the shots until he came to the right ones. He handed it over to his old friend.

Mr. Pederson's face filled with wonder as he viewed one photograph after another.

"Amazing," he said. "There are creatures here that no one knows anything about." He clicked through several more. "Incredible. *Stygimoloch* in action. I always wondered what their thickened skulls were used for. Do you know how extraordinary these photos are?" He suddenly turned to Mildred and Daniel.

Their eyes sparkled in acknowledgment. "This will fuel and direct my research for years!"

"Our research," Mildred said.

"Wait until you see all the things we collected." Daniel stopped, his shoulders drooping. "Except, we had to leave Dr. Roost's pack behind. Almost everything was in it."

Dr. Roost looked as forlorn as Daniel felt. Then she said, "Never mind. We have a lot of it up here." She pointed to her head. "We'll just need to jot it down before we forget. The pictures will help."

"I have a few things in my notebook," admitted Daniel, "but only some maps, and notes, measurements, and sketches of the *Edmontosaurus*."

"Well, at least that's something," Pederson said. He continued looking at the photos, constantly amazed by the number of species they'd captured.

Craig looked over his shoulder, totally enthralled. "Do you think I could learn how to do the kind of work you do?"

"I don't see why not," Mr. Pederson said. "In fact, I could help you get started. Of course, you'd have years of study ahead of you."

"I'll find a way somehow!" Craig vowed.

"Excellent! I'll be looking forward to having you in the field," said Pederson, rising and handing the camera over to Craig. "Many paleontologists get started by volunteering and doing work just like you are right now. Did you know it was an amateur that discovered Scotty, the *Tyrannosaurus rex* at Eastend?"

"Really?" Craig bubbled over with enthusiasm.

"I could lend you some of my books too," Daniel offered.

"Thanks." Craig beamed at them, as Mildred Roost chuckled.

Pederson headed over to his little hotplate and turned it on to heat some water for tea.

"So what's going on back at the farm and the dig?" asked Daniel, still fishing for information.

"Why don't you just come out and ask what you want to know?" said Craig with a teasing grin. "No, no one knows where you are. Todd and I covered for you. He's back at the farm right now, helping your dad with the haying. Your dad said he's a good worker and he might be able to hire him for a few days."

"Awesome!" Daniel answered. "Then will you continue helping at the dig?"

"Sure!" Craig answered. "Being fed by your mom is payment enough for me!"

They all laughed.

"So what's happening with the tourists?"

"Lindsay and Jed have the hikes covered and the tours to the quarry don't start for a while yet."

"Thanks!" Daniel said, relieved. He wouldn't be totally off the hook with his parents, but at least they weren't overly concerned about where he was.

"By the way, young man," Pederson came over and stared down at Daniel. "I don't ever want you to time travel again!"

"Well, but I didn't do it on purpose to start with," stammered Daniel.

"No, but this last time you did." Pederson shook his head. "I don't even want to think about what could have happened to you. Did you ever think about what it would do to your parents if you simply disappeared?"

Daniel stared down at his feet, not knowing what to say. He realized he actually hadn't considered their feelings or what they would think or do if he never came back. He'd only reacted to the sheer excitement and wonder of the opportunity to time travel.

"You have great parents. They love you very much. I want you to think about them too."

"That's true, Daniel," Craig said. "You don't know how lucky you are. You have a wonderful mother and a dad who treats you nice."

"You're right, Mr. Pederson," said Daniel, quietly. He had a great deal to think about. He didn't want to hurt anyone. His mother, his dad, even Cheryl would be crushed if he disappeared.

"I would be devastated too if you time travelled again and didn't come back. How could I ever face your parents, knowing the truth and not being able to do anything about it?" Pederson's eyes glistened as he spoke.

Daniel suddenly realized how much he meant to Mr. Pederson and how close he felt to this special old man, as if Pederson were his grandfather. He really was old and vulnerable, thought Daniel, recalling how he'd panicked when he'd come across Mr. Pederson lying prone at the quarry, and he was alone. Daniel slipped an arm around Mr. Pederson's waist and gave him a quick squeeze.

Daniel understood what Ole Pederson was saying about being aware of other people's reactions, but he also knew how important these trips were. Maybe he could go again when he was older. Or maybe he could figure out ways to make it safe. Daniel glanced over at Craig and saw that he was probably thinking the same thing.

When he stepped back, Daniel said, "I sure appreciate what you've said, sir, but I think what we're accomplishing is important too."

"It certainly is, lad," agreed Pederson. "But it's just too dangerous for you or anyone else to go there again."

"But these trips are too important to give up," Craig broke in. "Just imagine what else could be discovered."

"We could take proper equipment next time," Daniel offered. "There must be a way to make it safer to go."

"Now whoa, boys. Let's not get carried away. For you, there is no next time!"

"I agree, Ole. There's no way they should be going anywhere near there again," Dr. Roost interjected. "But it might be okay for you and me to go, because we're old and don't really have anyone who'd be hurt if we never came back."

"*I'd* be hurt if you didn't come back!" Daniel stared from one to the other.

"I don't have any family, but what about your son and grandchildren?" Pederson asked Mildred.

"I don't see them much anyway and they expect me to die some day," she said.

Pederson objected. "None of us should be going, least of all you, Daniel. If something happened to you, I couldn't forgive myself."

Daniel could see the struggle within his old friend, the helplessness he felt, and the guilt he'd dwell on if they never returned.

"The question is academic anyway," said Mildred. "Daniel dropped the cone. We had to leave it behind to get home. There is no mechanism for getting back."

Daniel nodded sadly. Then he remembered the pre-historic leaf in his notebook. He glanced around to see if anyone had noticed his reaction, but Mr. Pederson was busy making the tea and Mildred was rearranging herself in the chair. Craig, however, watched him intently.

Daniel sat poker-faced, not daring to speak or make any movement that would confirm Craig's suspicions. Then Craig raised his eyebrow and Daniel knew Craig had realized there was a way for them to travel again. He also knew Craig wouldn't say anything.

Pederson arrived with the tea and began distributing teacups around his small wooden table. He poured a cup for Dr. Roost and rested it within easy reach for her.

"So Daniel, let's have a look at that notebook of yours. I'd love to see the sketches of the *Edmontosaurus*."

Daniel hesitated, just for a moment. He couldn't let anyone see the notebook until he'd removed the leaf, but he couldn't do that with everyone watching him. Before he could figure out what to do, the room became quiet. He looked up to find everyone staring at him.

In the stunned silence that followed, Daniel tried to cover up his blunder, but it was no use.

"You have something that will transport you back to the past again, don't you?" Dr. Roost jabbed him with her cane.

"Daniel?" Mr. Pederson stared at him intently. "Is this true?"

Daniel nodded reluctantly.

"Then we really could go." Pederson looked at Mildred.

Dr. Roost's eyes lit up. "We'd have the research trip of a lifetime."

Daniel shook his head. "Oh no you don't! This last trip was bad enough."

"If you're going, I'm going too," Craig piped up.

"No one's going!" declared Daniel. There was no way he wanted to let the old couple go on their own, nor Craig. And he sure wasn't ready to go again.

"Of course not, Daniel," agreed Mr. Pederson. "We have plenty of material to study right now, and it is too dangerous for any of us to go. It's totally out of the question."

"Exactly," Daniel said.

Everyone sipped at their tea, lost in their own thoughts. Dr. Roost and Ole Pederson snuck glances at one another with little smiles. Craig picked up the camera again, scanning through the images.

While everyone was distracted, Daniel tucked his notebook into his backpack. He had to think of somewhere safe to tuck the leaf away. Until then he wasn't willing to open the notebook again. He was too exhausted to even think about the possibility of returning to the past.

Ole Pederson broke the quiet, "But to see the dinosaurs…"

Mildred cut him off. "We'll see." She patted his hand.

Daniel sighed.

VOCABULARY/DESCRIPTIONS

The material about paleontology found throughout this novel comes mostly from the Cretaceous Period. A brief description of some of the terms used follows, with their pronunciations. The Frenchman River Valley, where this story takes place, is located in the southwest area of Saskatchewan.

TERMS

CRETACEOUS PERIOD *(cree-TAY-shus):*
The Cretaceous Period, 146 to 65 million years ago, was the latter part of the Mesozoic era when great dinosaurs roamed the land and huge flying reptiles ruled the skies. A variety of smaller mammals and creatures also populated the earth and seas. The world was one of tropical temperatures all year round. Flowering plants and trees made their first widespread appearance, creating bright, beautiful places with their reds, yellows, and purples.

Before that time, there were only the browns and greens of trees and ferns and the blues of the skies and seas.

NOTE: *Creta is the Latin word for chalk. The Cretaceous Period is named for the chalky rock from southeastern England that was the first Cretaceous Period sediment studied.*

K-T MASS EXTINCTION:

K-T stands for Cretaceous-Tertiary. "K" is for Kreide – a German word meaning chalk, the sediment layer from that time. "T" is for Tertiary, the geological period that followed the Cretaceous Period. About 65 million years ago, it is believed that all land animals over 25 kg (55 pounds) went extinct, as well as many smaller organisms. This included the obliteration of the dinosaurs, pterosaurs, large sea creatures like the plesiosaurs and mosasaurs, as well as ammonites, some bird families, and various fishes and other marine species. There are many theories as to why this mass extinction occurred, but many scientists favour the one of an extraterrestrial body, a meteor, or asteroid hitting the earth.

PALEONTOLOGY *(PAY-lee-on-TALL-o-gee):*
Paleontology is the branch of geology and biology that deals with the prehistoric forms of life through the study of plant and animal fossils.

TERTIARY PERIOD *(TUR-sheer-ee):*
The Tertiary Period is the name for a portion of the most recent geological era known as the Cenozoic Era, also known as the "Age of Mammals," which lasted from about 65 to 2 million years ago. The term Tertiary was coined about the middle of the eighteenth century and refers to a particular layer of sedimentary deposits. Many mammals developed during that time, including primitive whales, rodents, pigs, cats, rhinos, and others familiar to us today.

CREATURES MENTIONED IN THE BOOK

Ankylosaurs (AN-kye-loh-sawrs):
A group of armoured, plant-eating dinosaurs that existed from the mid-Jurassic to the late Cretaceous Periods. *Ankylosaurus* was a huge armoured dinosaur, measuring about 7.5 to 10.7 m (25 to 35 feet) long, 1.8 m (6 feet) wide and 1.2 m (4 feet) tall; it weighed roughly 3 to 4 tonnes. Its entire top side was heavily protected from carnivores with thick, oval plates embedded (fused) in its leathery skin, 2 rows of spikes along its body, large horns that projected from the back of the head, and a club-like tail. It even had bony plates as protection for its eyes. Only its under-belly was unplated. Flipping it over was the only way to wound it.

BASILEMYS *(BAH-zil-emm-ees):*
A tortoise-like creature with a shell up to 1.5 m (5 feet) across. This is the largest known fossil turtle from the Frenchman River Valley.

BOREALOSUCHUS *(BOR-ee-al-o-such-us):*
A crocodile in existence in the late Cretaceous Period in Saskatchewan. This crocodile would be little compared to its earlier ancestors, about 2 to 3 m (7 to 10 feet) in length. It would run from a *T. rex,* as opposed to taking it head-on like the larger crocodiles would have.

CHAMPOSAURUS *(CHAMP–oh–SAWR-us):*
Most of the champosaurs are fairly small, reaching only about 1.5 m (5 feet) in length, but some specimens measuring over 3 m (10 feet) in length have been recently found in North Dakota. They had long, narrow jaws with fine, pointed teeth, and closely resemble the modern gavial of India. They may look like crocodiles, but are not closely related to them. Champosaurs fed on fish, snails, mollusks, and turtles. They lived in Saskatchewan from about 75 million years ago to about 55 million years ago.

CIMOLOPTERYX *(sim-oh-LOP-ter-icks)* ("Cretaceous wing"):
An early bird resembling typical shorebirds of today and found in the late Cretaceous Period in Saskatchewan. This bird had a long, slender bill and long, strong legs for

wading and running. It probably probed in the sand or mud for food.

CORYTHOSAURUS *(co-RITH-oh-SAWR-us)* ("Helmet lizard"):
Corythosaurus was a large plant-eating duck-billed dinosaur that probably fed on palm leaves, pine needles, seeds, cycad ferns, twigs, magnolia leaves and fruit. It may have weighed up to 5 tonnes and was about 2 m (7 feet) tall at the hips and 9 to 10 m (30 to 33 feet) long. (NB: Corythosaurs are known from slightly older sediments.)

DROMAEOSAURUS *(DRO-mee-o-SAWR-us)* ("fast-running lizard"):
Dromaeosaurus was a small, fast, meat-eating, theropod dinosaur with sickle-like toe claws, sharp teeth, and big eyes. It lived during the late Cretaceous Period and was about 1.8 m (6 feet) long, weighing roughly 15 kg (33 pounds). It was a very smart, deadly dinosaur and may have hunted in packs. Fossils have been found in Alberta, Saskatchewan, and Montana.

EDMONTOSAURUS *(ed-MON-toh-SAWR-us)* ("Edmonton [rock formation] lizard"):
A large, plant-eating member of the duckbill dinosaurs, or hadrosaurs that lived about 73 to 65 million years ago in the Cretaceous Period in western North America. It had hundreds of teeth crowded together in the huge jaw,

enabling it to eat tough leaves and other vegetation. This flat-headed duckbill grew to about 13 m (42 feet) in length and weighed 3.1 tonnes. It may have had anywhere from 800 to 1,600 teeth. *Edmontosaurus Saskatchewanensis*, named in 1926 by Sternberg, is the only identified species of *Edmontosaurus* so far found in Saskatchewan.

GARFISH (A.S. gar, "spear"):
Garfish is a name commonly given to certain fishes with long, narrow bodies and bony, sharp-toothed beaks. Primarily freshwater fish, today the largest tropical gar reach lengths of about 3.7 m (12.1 feet). They are a primitive fish that have existed for millions of years. They have needle-like teeth, a dorsal fin that sits far back on the heavily scaled body. They are able to breathe in stagnant water, and their roe is poisonous to many animals, including humans.

HADROSAURS *(HAD-roh-SAWRS)* ("bulky lizards"):
Hadrosaurs were a family of duck-billed dinosaurs that ranged from 7 to 10 m (23 to 42 feet) long and lived in the late Cretaceous Period. They appear to have been highly social creatures, laying eggs in nests communally. Nests with eggs have been found in both Alberta and Montana. The only known hadrosaur in Saskatchewan is the *Edmontosaurus saskatchewanensis* (see description above).

HESPERORNIS *(HES-per-OR-nis)* ("western bird"):
Hesperornithids were a family of large flightless birds that

swam in the oceans of the late Cretaceous and preyed on small fish. They have been found in the Upper Cretaceous of Western Kansas and Saskatchewan. It is likely that they swam and fed much like modern penguins. They were also apparently limited to the Northern Hemisphere, much like penguins are limited to the Southern Hemisphere today.

IGUANODON *(ig-WAHN-oh-don)* ("Iguana Tooth"):
The Iguanodon was a relatively fast plant eating dinosaur that ranged to about 6 to 11 m (30 feet) long, 4 to 5 m (16 feet) tall and weighed 4.5 to 5.5 tonnes. It was a herding animal that could run on two legs or walk on four and is said to have run at least 15 to 20 km/hr. It had a horny, toothless beak, three-toed feet with hoof-like claws, and a conical thumb spike on each hand that served as a weapon of defense. Some scientists think it had a long tongue like a giraffe and that it was extremely intelligent. The Iguanodon lived in the early Cretaceous Period, which was about 110 to 135 million years ago.

MOSASAURS *(MOES-ah-SAWRS):*
Mosasaurs were a group of giant, lizard-like marine reptiles that extended 12.5 to 17.6 metres (40 to 59 feet) long. They were not dinosaurs, but may be related to snakes and monitor lizards. They were powerful swimmers, adapted to living in shallow seas. These carnivores (meat-eaters) still breathed air. A short-lived line of reptiles,

they became extinct during the K-T extinction, 65 million years ago.

PLESIOSAURS *(plee-zee-oh-SAWRS)* ("near lizard"):
Plesiosaurs were not dinosaurs. They were flippered marine reptiles from the Mesozoic Era. Plesiosaurs are divided into two groups: the *Plesiosauroids* had long, snake-like necks, tiny heads, and wide bodies; while the *Pliosauroids* had large heads with very strong jaws and short necks.

PTERANODONS *(tair-AH-no-dons):*
Pteranodons were large members of the pterosaur family from the Cretaceous Period. They were not dinosaurs, but flying prehistoric reptiles, toothless hunters who scooped up fish from the seas. They were about 1.8 m (6 feet) long, had a 7.8 m (25 foot) wingspan.

PTERODACTYLUS *(ter-oh-DAK-til-us)* ("winged finger"):
This small flying, prehistoric reptile, a member of the pterosaurs group, had a wingspan that spread up to .75 m (2.5 feet). The wing was made up of skin stretched along the body between the hind limb and a very long fourth digit of the forelimb. It lived during the late Jurassic Period.

PTEROSAURS *(TER-o-SAWRS)* ("winged lizards"):
Flying reptiles that included Pteranodons and

Pterodactyls, they were the largest vertebrates ever known to fly. They lived from the Jurassic to the Cretaceous Period.

PURGATORIUS *(pur-ga-TOR-ee-us):*
A small, rodent-sized mammal from the Cretaceous Period, which may have been about ten cm (4 inches) long, probably weighed no more than 20 g (¾ ounce), and fed on insects. Some have suggested that this mammal may have been the earliest primate known.

"SCOTTY":
The *T. rex* found near Eastend, Saskatchewan in 1991.

QUAESITOSAURUS *(kway-ZEE-tuh-SAWR-us)* ("abnormal or extraordinary lizard"):
This long-necked, whip-tailed plant-eater had good hearing. It lived about 80 to 85 million years ago, probably eating conifer tree leaves, gingkos, seed ferns, cycads, ferns, club mosses, and horsetails with their peg-like teeth. It was about 20 to 23 m long (66 to 75 feet), and had a long skull, a wide snout and a large ear opening.

STEGOCERAS *(STEG-oh-CEER-us)* ("roofed horn"):
A bipedal, herbivorous, dome-headed, plant-eating dinosaur from the late Cretaceous Period about 76 to 65 million years ago. It was about 2 m (7 feet) long and lived in what is now Alberta, Canada. (Not to be confused with

a *Stegosaurus [pronounced STEG-oh-SAWR-us],* meaning "roof lizard," a plant-eating dinosaur with armoured plates along its back and tall spikes that lived during the Jurassic Period, about 156 to 150 million years ago.)

STYGIMOLOCH *(STIJ-eh-MOLL-uk)* (demon from the river Styx):
Stygimoloch was a thick-skulled plant-eating dinosaur (a pachycephalosaur) that walked on two legs. It was only 2 to 3 m (7 to 10 feet) long, and weighed about 50 to 75 kg (110 to 165 pounds). This unusual-looking dinosaur had bony spikes and bumps on its skull; the many horns ranged up to 100 mm (4 inches) long. Pachycephalosaurs probably engaged in head-butting both as a defense against predators and during rivalry with others of their own species.

THESCELOSAURUS *(THES-ke-loh-SAWR-us)* ("Marvellous lizard"):
This plant-eating dinosaur had a small head, a bulky body that was 3 to 4 m long, and less than 1 m (3 feet) tall at the hips. A member of the ceratopsian group, it also had a long, pointed tail and shorter arms and could probably run at about 50 km/hr for an extended time. Two partial skeletons have been found in Saskatchewan.

TOROSAURUS *(TOR-oh-SAW-rus)* ("pierced lizard"):
Torosaurus had a strong toothless beak that was able to

handle the toughest vegetation including small branches. A member of the ceratopsian group, it had a fierce appearance due to the two brow horns on its enormous 2.5 m (8 foot) skull, a short nose horn, and a long-frilled crest. Its powerful front legs were shorter than its hind legs, which gave it a very stable posture. *Torosaurus* could chew well with its cheek teeth. It lived about 70 to 65 million years ago. Fossils have been found in Wyoming, Montana, Colorado, South Dakota, New Mexico, Texas, and Utah (USA), and in Saskatchewan (Canada).

TRICERATOPS *(tri–SER–uh–tops):*
Triceratops was a rhinoceros-like dinosaur with a bony neck frill that lived about 72 to 65 million years ago. From the ceratopsian group, this plant-eater was about 8 m (26 feet) long, 3 m (10 feet) tall, and weighed from 6 to 12 tonnes. A relatively slow dinosaur, it had three horns on its head and a set of powerful jaws. Its parrot-like beak held many cheek teeth. It had a short, pointed tail, a bulky body, and columnar legs with hoof-like claws. Many Triceratops fossils have been found, mostly in the western United States and in western Canada, including Saskatchewan.

TROODON *(TROH–oh–don):*
A very smart, human-sized, meat-eating dinosaur from the late Cretaceous Period. Fossils of *Troodon* have been found in Montana and Wyoming (USA), and Alberta

and Saskatchewan (Canada). It may have been one of the smartest dinosaurs, because it had a large brain compared to its body size.

TYRANNOSAURUS REX *(tye-RAN-oh-SAWR-us recks or Tie-ran-owe-saw-rus-recks)* ("tyrant lizard king"):
A huge, meat-eating theropod dinosaur from the late Cretaceous Period. The largest meat-eater that has ever existed, it stood 5 to 7 m (16 to 21 feet) tall on its great clawed feet and had terrible, dagger-like teeth, 15 cm (6 inches) long. *Tyrannosaurus rex* was roughly 5 to 7 tonnes in weight. Its enormous skull was about 1.5 m (5 feet) long. The eye sockets in its skull are 10.2 cm (4 inches) across; its eyeballs would have been about 7.6 cm (3 inches) in diameter.

ZAPSALIS (ZAP-sa-lis) ("through shears"):
A meat-eating dinosaur (a theropod) that lived during the Cretaceous Period. This theropod was found in the Judith River Formation, Montana, USA in 1876. It is only known through its teeth and is currently classified as a troodontid.

OTHER REFERENCES & NOTES

BEES:
Over the past three years, Stephen Hasiotic, a Colorado University doctoral student and geology lab instructor, has found nests, almost identical to modern honeybee nests, that date back 207 to 220 million years, or about twice as far back as the oldest fossils of flowering plants. This means bees have been around longer than previously thought. The ancient bees could have found sugars and nutrients – which they find today in the nectar of flowers – in coniferous plants or even in animal carcasses.

RECEPTACULITES *(REE-sep-TACK- you-light-eeze):*
Receptaculites are often referred to as the "sunflower coral" and date from 450 million years ago. At one time thought to be a sponge, it is commonly found as a flattened shape with a pattern of crossing lines like the head of a ripe sunflower. In more recent times, Receptaculites

are considered sponge-like rather than a true sponge. (NB: This invertebrate is from the Ordovician Age, and Daniel collected it a couple of years earlier from an entirely different spot than the Cretaceous Period finds they are working on currently.

CROCODILIANS:

Crocodilians are the order of archosaurs (ruling lizards) that includes alligators, crocodiles, gavials, etc. They evolved during the late Triassic Period and are a type of reptile.

DRAGONFLIES:

Dragonflies, primitive flying insects that can hover in the air, evolved during the Mississippian Period, about 360 to 325 million years ago. Huge dragonflies with wingspans up to 70 cm (27.5 inches) existed during the Mesozoic Era (when the dinosaurs lived).

BIBLIOGRAPHY

Bakker, Robert T., *Dinosaur Heresies*, Morrow, New York, 1986

Gross, Renie, *Dinosaur Country: Unearthing the Badlands' Prehistoric Past*, Western Producer Prairie Books, 1985, ISBN: 0-88833-121-5

Lauber, Patricia & Henderson, Douglas, *Living with Dinosaurs*, Bradbury Press, N.Y., 1991. ISBN: 0-02-754521-0

MacMillan Illustrated Encyclopedia of Dinosaurs and Prehistoric Animals, Editors: Dr. Barry Cox, Dr. Colin Harrison, Dr. R.J.G. Savage, Dr. Brian Gardiner, MacMillan London Ltd., 1988.

McIver, Elisabeth E., "The Paleoenvironment of Tyrannosaurus rex from Southwestern Saskatchewan, Canada," *Canadian Journal of Earth Sciences, #39* (2002), Pages: 207 – 221

Norman, David Ph. D., & Milner, Angela Ph. D., *Dinosaur,* Dorling Kindersley Ltd., 1989. ISBN 0-7894-5808-X

Parker, Steve, *Dinosaurs And How They Live*d, Macmillan of Canada, 1988. ISBN: 0-7715-96832-4 (Window on the World series)

Reid, Monty, *The Last Great Dinosaurs: An Illustrated Guide to Alberta's Dinosaurs,* Red Deer College Press, Red Deer, Alberta, 1990, ISBN: 0-88995-055-5.

Relf, Pat, *A Dinosaur Named Sue,* Scholastic, Inc. 2002. ISBN: 0-439-09985-4

Simpson, George Gaylord, *The Dechronization of Sam Magruder*, St. Martin's Griffin, New York, 1996. ISBN: 0-312-15514-X

Smith, Alan, *Saskatchewan Birds*, Lone Pine Publishing, 2001. ISBN: 1-55105-304-7

Stewart, Janet, *The Dinosaurs: A New Discovery,* Hayes Publishing Ltd., Burlington, Ontario, 1989, ISBN: 0-88625-235-0.

Storer, Dr. John, *Geological History of Saskatchewan,* Saskatchewan Museum of Natural History, Government of Saskatchewan, 1989.

Tokaryk, Tim T., *Blue Jay*, Archaeology: Puzzles of the Past, 52 (2), June, 1994

Tokaryk, Tim T., *Blue Jay*, Palaeontology: Treasures on the Shelves, 52 (3), September 1994

Tokaryk, Tim T., & Bryant, Harold N. *The Fauna from the* Tyrannosaurus rex *Excavation, Frenchman Formation (Late Maastrichtian), Saskatchewan,* as published in: Summary of Investigations, 2004, Vol. 1, Miscellaneous Report 2004-4.1, paper A-18. Vol 1. Saskatchewan Geological Survey, Regina.

Tokaryk, Tim T., *Saskatchewan Archaeological Society Newsletter*, Palaeontology News: "Encounters with Monsters," February, 1991, Vol 12, Number 1

Tokaryk, Tim T., *Saskatchewan Archaeological Society Newsletter*, Palaeontology News: "A Tale of Two Vertebrae," April 1992, Vol 13, Number 2

Tokaryk, Tim T., Saskatchewan Archaeological Society Newsletter, Palaeontology News: *Serendipity, Surprises and Monsters of the Deep, October, 1996,* Vol 17, Number 5
Tokaryk, Tim T., *Scotty's Dinosaur Delights, A Paleo Breakfast,* 1995. Friends of the Museum, Eastend, Saskatchewan.

Tokaryk, Tim T., *Preliminary Review of the Non-Mammalian Vertebrates from the Frenchman Formation (Late Maastrichtian) of Saskatchewan.* As published in: McKenzie-McAnally, L. (ed), Canadian Paleontology Conference Fields Trip Guidebook No 6. Upper Cretaceous and Tertiary Stratigraphy and Paleontology of Southern Saskatchewan, /1997. Geological Association of Canada.

Wallace, Joseph, *The Rise and Fall of the Dinosaur,* Michael Friedman Publishing Group, Inc., New York, N.Y., 1987, ISBN:0-8317-2368-8.

URLS:

http://www.dinocountry.com

http://www.enchantedlearning.com

http://www.dinodatabase.com/dinoclaso8.asp

http://teacher.scholastic.com/researchtools/articlearchives/dinos/general.htm

http://www.enchantedlearning.com/themes/dinos.shtml

http://www.enchantedlearning.com/subjects/dinosaurs/
activities/math/size.shtml

http://www.nps.gov/dino/dinos.htm

http://www.tiscali.co.uk/reference/dictionaries/animals/
data/m0049059.html

http://cas.bellarmine.edu/tietjen/images/
tropical_paradise_at_the_cretace.htm

Author's Web site:
http://www.judithsilverthorne.ca/

ACKNOWLEDGEMENTS

My profound thanks to Tim Tokaryk, paleontologist at the Royal Saskatchewan Museum field station in Eastend, for his many suggestions, and for keeping me on track in the world of paleontology. His patience and expertise is appreciated beyond measure. Thanks to Mark Caswell, Heather Gibson, and the staff at the *T. rex* Discovery Centre; and to Scott and Warren at the newest quarry site, and my guide Travis. Thank you again to all of you for sharing your wealth of information, which has made the writing of this book so much easier. I really appreciate being able to be as accurate as possible! Any errors are solely mine.

Thank you to Barbara Sapergia for her insightful and enthusiastic editing that contributed to the focus and polish of the manuscript. My heartfelt thanks go to Nik, Duncan, Karen, Deborah, and Melanie, a fabulous publishing team that I treasure highly and profoundly.

Thanks to Constable James Fraser of the RCMP for his valuable information and support. And thanks to everyone who contributed in any way to the details of this book.

I am especially grateful to my parents, Stan and Elaine Iles for their loving support and encouragement.

Patricia Miller-Schroeder, Susan McKenzie, Alison Lohans, Jan Johnston, and Neil Jones continually warm my heart with their dedicated support of my writing and their unconditional friendship.

ABOUT THE AUTHOR

Judith Silverthorne is the author of six previous books. Four of them are children's novels: *The Secret of the Stone House, The Secret of Sentinel Rock, Dinosaur Hideout,* and *Dinosaur Breakout.* The other two are non-fiction: a biography called *Made in Saskatchewan: Peter Rupchan, Ukrainian Pioneer and Potter* and *Ingrained Legacy: Saskatchewan Pioneer Woodworkers 1870-1930.* She has won the Saskatchewan Book Award for Children's Literature for her first two children's books and the last two have also been finalists. Her children's novels are also on the *Our Choice* recommendation lists of the Canadian Children's Book Centre. As well, *Dinosaur Hideout* was nominated for the 2004 Willow Awards.

She also works as an editor, curator, mentor, and instructor of writing and film courses. Silverthorne has lived most of her life in Saskatchewan, and is keenly interested in the landscape and history of the province, which inspires many of her works. She currently lives in Regina, where she juggles a full-time job with writing novels and extensive travel to do author presentations and workshops on the writing process. For more information, or to contact Ms. Silverthorne, please visit her Web site at: http://www.judithsilverthorne.ca.

TRAVEL BACK

WITH DANIEL FOR MORE DINOSAUR FUN

Check out the first two books in Judith Silverthorne's **Dinosaur Adventure Series:**

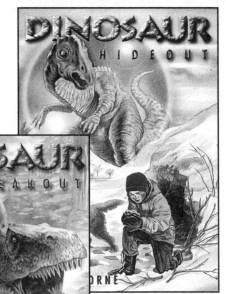

#1 Dinosaur Hideout
ISBN-13: 978-1-55050-226-8
ISBN-10: 1-55050-226-3
$7.95CAD/$6.95USD

#2 Dinosaur Breakout
ISBN-13: 978-1-55050-294-7
ISBN-10: 1-55050-294-8
$7.95CAD/$6.95USD

AVAILABLE AT FINE BOOKSELLERS EVERYWHERE.

Check out **www.coteaubooks.com** and Judith Silverthorne's Web site **www.judithsilverthorne.ca** for more information on the series.

Amazing stories. Amazing kids.